CALEB FINN

ARCHIVES of DESPAIR

PENGUIN BOOKS

PENGUIN BOOKS

UK | USA | Canada | Ireland | Australia
India | New Zealand | South Africa | China

Penguin Random House Australia is part of the Penguin Random House group of companies whose addresses can be found at global.penguinrandomhouse.com.

First published by Penguin Books, an imprint of Penguin Random House Australia Pty Ltd, in 2023

Cover and internal illustrations by Adam Parata
Cover design by Christa Moffitt, Christabella Designs
Author photograph by Caleb Finn
Internal design and typesetting by Midland Typesetters, Australia

Printed and bound in Australia by Griffin Press, an accredited ISO AS/NZS 14001 Environmental Management Systems printer

A catalogue record for this book is available from the National Library of Australia

ISBN 978 1 76 134169 4 (Paperback)

penguin.com.au

We at Penguin Random House Australia acknowledge that Aboriginal and Torres Strait Islander peoples are the Traditional Custodians and the first storytellers of the lands on which we live and work. We honour Aboriginal and Torres Strait Islander peoples' continuous connection to Country, waters, skies and communities. We celebrate Aboriginal and Torres Strait Islander stories, traditions and living cultures; and we pay our respects to Elders past and present.

ARCHIVES of DESPAIR

To my son,
Darkness is all around us,
And sometimes, there are monsters.
In the light, the monsters may be watching.
But in the dark, the monsters can't see you.

CONTENT WARNING

This book contains mentions of sensitive and potentially distressing themes that may be troubling to some readers. Including, but not limited to, references of death, derealisation, existential themes, body horror, vivid nightmare imagery, depictions of eating disorders and childhood trauma.

The author does not take these themes lightly and has written this book with adolescent readers in mind. His hope for these stories is to encourage younger readers to face their fears and persevere through confronting situations.

Please be mindful of these and other possible triggers, and seek resources, if needed, on page 231.

EMAIL RECEIVED!

FROM: <HELLO@████████.COM>

WE HAVE BEEN WATCHING YOU AND WE WANT TO HELP.

I REPRESENT A PRIVATE ORGANISATION SEEKING INFORMATION.

IT SEEMS WE SHARE A COMMON GOAL OF FINDING THE TRUTH.

AS THE SAYING GOES: THE ENEMY OF MY ENEMY IS MY FRIEND.

THE ARC IS THE ENEMY. THE ARC HAS THE ANSWERS.

WE REQUIRE YOUR ASSISTANCE AND WISH TO COLLABORATE.

USER: WAKE
PASSWORD: AJFY386!

WE WILL CONTACT YOU AGAIN ONCE YOU ARE IN THE ARCHIVES.

****

PREPARING TO BOOT SYSTEM . . . DONE
PREPARING USER INTERFACE . . . DONE

WELCOME TO THE ARC DATABASE!
USER: WAKE
PASSWORD: AJFY386!

WELCOME BACK, DR ROBERT WAKE
/scan directory: ARCHIVES_OF_DESPAIR
ARCHIVE INTEGRITY 82% . . .
10 ENTRIES FOUND . . .
/open entries

CONTENTS

WHITE WALLS 1
HAPPY BIRTHDAY 23
PLEASE DON'T GO 47
FLAT GRANNY 63
PRETEND PEOPLE 93
MS CACKLE 127
I'M NOT KEVIN 143
LOVELY DAY 163
185
199

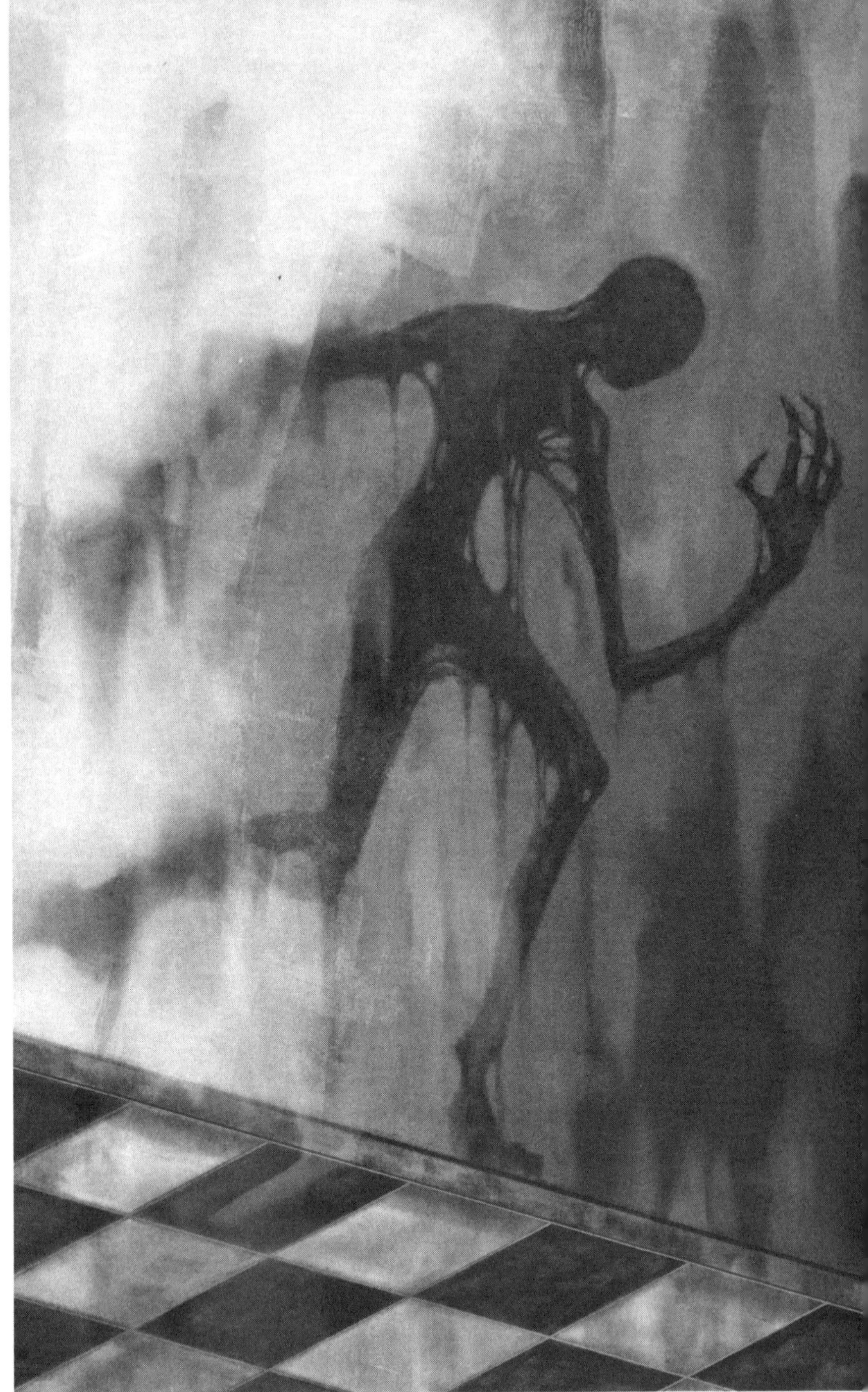

WHITE WALLS

'You're still here, Jerry.'

The voice echoed from the small, dark kitchen across the room. Sitting on my dad's office chair, I spun around towards the man calling his name.

Though everything was a blur from spinning so quickly, I could tell it was The Cleaner, wearing the same blue jumpsuit and matching cap as always. The same unkempt, bushy moustache and same mop in hand as he scrubbed away at the pristine kitchen tiles.

'I'm nearly done, I promise. Just finishing up here and then taking this little lady out for a treat,' Dad replied, trying to pat around the tight ponytail on my head. Mum wanted me to look tidy for my school photo.

I caught my foot on the wheel to stop myself spinning.

'I was in the school paper!' I beamed at The Cleaner, still trying to focus my eyes and keep my head straight.

'Yep! That's right! My little girl got on the front page of

the school paper for winning gold! Can you believe that? The fastest thirteen-year-old in school.'

I looked up at Dad to see his proud face looking down at me.

The Cleaner continued staring from a distance, remaining silent.

'So I think it's only fair that the kiddo deserves some –'

'DOUGH-nuts!' I boasted, cutting Dad off.

It had been a boring afternoon since school ended. As usual, I had to wait for Dad to finish working before we could leave. It wouldn't be so bad if there was just something *to do.*

Not to mention the nauseating smell of paint that overpowered every other scent in the building.

'Jerry, you know *the rules,*' The Cleaner replied, holding his unflinching gaze. An awkward pause stifled the air as the smile disappeared from Dad's face, his hands drooping to his sides.

'Yeah, sure, sure. We'll be out of your hair in just a second. I've just got some papers to drop off on the third floo–'

'Time is up, Jerry.'

Dad paused before quickly gathering the last of his paperwork and turning off the desk lamp. Grabbing his briefcase, he gestured at me to follow him out of his office. I jumped off the chair, still a little dizzy. The world felt crooked as my walk turned into a run. I felt myself beginning to lose balance, crashing into the doorframe.

'Whoa, be careful, kiddo,' Dad said, catching my fall. 'You nearly touched the walls. You know they're wet.'

I clung onto Dad as I planted both feet on the floor. Brushing myself off, I noticed that another pair of feet were right in front of me.

I slowly looked up, first noticing little white blots of paint against the blue jumpsuit, then The Cleaner's face towering over me. Even though the cap was covering his face, I could feel his eyes boring into mine. He let out a single, long exhale directly into my face.

His breath could only be described as a mix of strong cleaning chemicals and a smell that I couldn't quite place, but it reminded me of my grandma's funeral last year. Something about that stench threw me right back into that awful memory.

I cautiously stepped back as my dad grabbed my elbow, shuffling me out the door.

'Let's go, kiddo,' Dad whispered in my ear as we walked hastily out of his office and down the hallway.

Dad's gentle but firm hand pressed against my back as we walked. I looked around at the stark white walls. It always made me uncomfortable just how *white* the office was. I found it odd since every other floor of the building had black walls.

The white walls matched the white ceiling, and the flickering fluorescent lights above gave me a headache if I stared at them for too long. The only colour left in the building belonged to the orange, patterned carpet that stretched and weaved through the offices and corridors.

As we walked down the long, seemingly endless hallway, I searched my memory for a time when the walls *weren't* being painted. I'd been coming here every day after school for the last few weeks and yet, the walls were *always* being painted.

I've heard the saying 'wet paint never dries', or was it 'a watched kettle never whistles?' Was it a pot? No, it had to –

Clang.

The sudden noise snapped me from my thoughts and directed my attention behind me. It was The Cleaner standing in the doorframe we had just come out of, mop in hand. We were already halfway down the hallway, but I could still see water from the mop dripping down his hand and onto the carpet.

'Look, I told you. I'll be in and out. I know it's past seven, but you know the boss will have my head if the paperwork isn't on his desk by tomorrow.'

Clang.

Again, The Cleaner smacked the wooden handle of the mop against the doorframe. The hairs on my neck stood up as The Cleaner continued to stand motionless.

What is he trying to tell us? Is he mad at Dad? Mad at me for nearly touching the walls?

Dad patted my back as he started jogging back down the hallway towards The Cleaner.

I squinted and observed the conversation from afar.

I wish I was better at lip-reading. Having subtitles on while watching movies has really dampened my abilities, especially in this situation.

Rip.

A sound, reminiscent of tape ripping, caught my ears. It wasn't coming from the direction of Dad, but from behind me. I whipped my head around and tried to focus on the mind-numbingly white walls. The fluorescent lights above dissolved any shadows, making it hard to see where hallways split off into each other.

I walked down the corridor and turned a corner, scanning the walls until a small black spot on the wall caught my attention.

Something about it felt so unnatural against the blinding white.

What's so unusual about this black spot? Normally, I wouldn't think twice about it, but here? Where the walls were always so white? It piqued my interest.

I took one last look at Dad, who was still talking to The Cleaner, before disappearing around the corner again. I bent down and looked closer at the black spot.

What I thought was a spot of paint or a scuff mark, was instead a black *something* jutting straight out. It wasn't quite flat enough to be paper but could be easily mistaken for it. I ran my finger over it and watched it spring back to its position. Whatever it was had a slightly bumpy feel . . . and it was *warm*. The cogs turning in my head came to a screeching halt as I tried to make sense of what I was touching.

I tugged on the black *thing* and watched as it started to separate from the wall, pulling the white paint along with it.

The sound of paint ripping made me a little anxious that Dad would hear, but my curiosity got the better of me.

It's okay, I told myself. *No one's going to know.*

That's when I noticed that the wall underneath the *thing* was completely black. White paint slowly coloured my fingers as I toyed with the strip. It twisted and turned with ease as it slipped around in my fingers.

Rip.

There it was again. That tape ripping sound. It had definitely come from further down the hallway.

Another tiny *thing* was jutting from the wall, casting a small shadow underneath it.

Was the paint really that cheap? Is this why they need to paint the walls every day?

Rip. Rip. Rip.

That same noise! I strained my eyes to find where it was coming from. I couldn't tell if my mind was playing tricks on my unfocused eyes, but I could swear that the corridor walls were . . . *moving*. Just slightly.

I didn't like this.

Cold sweat dripped down my spine as I stared intensely at the wall, scanning for the slightest movements. Something was wrong.

Dad. Where's Dad? Stand up. Find Dad. I just want to go home.

My thoughts were running a million miles an hour as my breath began to quicken.

Instinctively, my body began to move, my mind slowly catching up to my legs as I nervously shuffled back towards the bend of the hall. I didn't dare look back as the ripping became more frequent. The faint change in white came into view, signalling that the corner was just ahead. I hoped Dad would be on the other side to make everything better. It was just a little further now . . .

CRASH.

A person standing behind the corner blocked my path, sending me backwards onto the floor. I hit my head against the carpet.

'Dad!' I called in a daze. The fluorescent lights blinded my eyes. All I could make out was a figure towering over me. I closed my eyes and latched onto the legs standing in front of me.

'Dad, I just wanna go home. I miss Mum. Please. Please.'

I expected Dad would've hugged me or comforted me by now, but he just stood still.

And there it was. That smell again.

The strong stench of chemicals burned my nose. I scrunched my face in disgust, desperately trying to blow the air back out of my nose.

The memory of Grandma's funeral filled my head. The closed casket, the stale air, the smell of the sterile waiting room that would forever be associated with her death.

I opened my eyes and stared at the white-speckled blue jumpsuit. I looked up at the familiar moustache and the eyes still obscured by the cap.

The overwhelming smell, combined with shock, made me recoil. The Cleaner remained completely motionless as I trembled beneath him.

'Where's Dad?' I asked sternly, desperately trying to mask my fear.

The Cleaner stayed silent, refusing to answer.

I peeked behind The Cleaner's legs to find a glimpse of Dad, but all I could see was the bright, white hallway leading down to Dad's office.

He must have just forgotten something, I rationalised to myself.

I grimaced at The Cleaner before jumping to my feet and sprinting down the hallway.

'Dad? Dad, where are you?!'

The lump in my throat grew as my call echoed through his empty office. The leather briefcase on the desk caught my eye, granting me a sliver of hope that Dad was still here.

He wouldn't leave without me. He wouldn't!

Tears began welling up as my mind conjured an image of the last time I saw Dad. It didn't make sense. There was only one way back to the elevator. There was no other explanation, he had to be here.

I turned around and looked down the hallway, catching a small glimpse of The Cleaner before he disappeared around the corner.

'Hey!' I cried out. 'Where's Dad?! What did you do to him?'

I launched into a sprint to catch up with The Cleaner. I was the fastest girl in my grade. If there's one thing I could count on, it was my speed.

I grabbed the corner and pushed my weight off the opposite wall, nearly losing my grip against the wet paint slipping through my fingers.

'Don't walk away from –'

My eyes widened; I couldn't finish my sentence.

Panic set in. Things just weren't making sense.

The Cleaner was gone, leaving me alone in the endless, white corridor.

But something was different.

I looked at the wall where I'd just seen the black paper-thin *thing*. It wasn't small anymore.

In its place was a tall black silhouette. It looked human-sized, but not like any human I'd seen before. It had the shape of a head, two arms and two legs, but the proportions were all wrong. The legs were too long, the arms were too crooked and the head was too thin. It was as if a person had been flattened under a steamroller or squeezed out through a tube of toothpaste.

Whatever had been painted into the wall wasn't there anymore.

I want to curl up into a ball and wake up from this nightmare, but I know I can't. Dad taught me better than to give into fear. I am going to get out of here. I fought against my body's instinct to freeze and focused on moving my feet. It took all my mental strength to just *move.*

But which way? Do I risk sprinting back to the elevator? Maybe I could hide in a cupboard and wait? I was out of time to think. I just need to move.

C'mon, you stupid feet. Move. MOVE.

I snapped out of my trance and whirled around, sprinting back down the hallway to Dad's office.

The windows. Someone must be able to see me, we're not that far off the ground. I can try and flag someone down to come save me and this will all be a distant memory.

I narrowly avoided Dad's desk as I scooted around to the windows. My eyes darted back and forth for someone on the ground, *anyone*.

A street lamp illuminated the rainy street, revealing the figure of a man walking towards a bus stop. He didn't seem to mind the light rain as he casually strolled towards the covered bus shelter.

I started to bang on the windows with all the strength I could muster.

'Help me! Please! Help!' I cried. White handprints began to smother the glass, but that was the least of my worries.

After what felt like an eternity of banging and screaming, the man looked up. A wave of excitement washed over me.

'Hey, up here! There's something in here!'

I knew the man couldn't hear me, but it didn't matter. All I could do now was wait anxiously for the man to react.

C'mon, c'mon.

I watched as the man took one hand out of his pocket and reached towards his head, tipping the brim of his bowler hat.

'What?! I'm not saying hello! I need –'

Rip.

That noise again. It was that *thing*, I knew it. I ducked behind Dad's desk, staring straight down the hallway. Whatever it was, it was coming.

I didn't dare look away as a shadow stretched across the wall. A long, bent leg appeared from the blur of white, followed by a crooked arm, along with the rest of the *thing*'s poor imitation of a human body. Raspy breaths gasping for air filled the silence as the *thing* walked its crippled body towards me. Its gaunt limbs cracked and squeaked as they moved in unnatural directions, barely propelling it forward. Globs of white paint fell to the carpet, revealing the thing's wet, black skin underneath.

It was coming straight towards me, and I had trapped myself in my dad's office. I had nowhere to go. I stumbled back, pulling myself up to glance again outside the window.

The man with the bowler hat was gone. I *definitely* didn't remember a bus pulling up.

I looked back down to see the thing continue to slowly writhe towards me. There was nowhere to hide, and Dad's desk wasn't going to save me for much longer.

Think, think, think.

The kitchen. It was the closest room and had plenty of cupboards to hide in. It was my best shot at getting out of here; *alive* at least. The thing was certainly going to see me, but it was my only option to avoid getting captured . . . *Or eaten.*

I set myself into a runner's stance and swallowed my fear, moving one foot then another, and then I was off. The distance was easy to clear, but I didn't dare look at the thing hobbling towards me (the sound itself was enough to give me nightmares).

I heel-turned into the dark kitchen, using my last precious seconds to feel around for the light switch.

Click. Click. Click. The room didn't get any brighter. I was going to have to feel my way to a hiding place. I could start to make out small details as my eyes slowly adjusted to the darkness. One of the walls seemed darker than the rest – it may have been my eyes playing tricks, but there was definitely something off about it. *Did The Cleaner miss some paint on the wall?*

Drip. Drip. Drip. In between my shallow breaths, the dripping tap helped me to find the closest cupboard and a chance of escaping this horror with my life.

The shadow in the doorway grew larger. I knew it was only a matter of seconds before the *thing* would get me.

I threw open the cupboard door and tossed the cleaning supplies onto the floor, squeezing myself inside the cramped space. It was tight, but I managed to fit inside, except for my leg. The sink drainpipe that ran through the cupboard clanged as I desperately threw my leg against it. It was no use. It wasn't going to fit.

'No, no, no, c'mon.'

Thud. Thud. Thud.

It was here. It was in the room. I was out of time. I had no choice but to leave the door ajar with my foot hanging slightly out and focus on covering my mouth with both hands.

It's fine. It's dark. It won't notice. Slow down. Remember your breathing techniques.

The sound of gasping and wheezing polluted the room.

My eyes struggled against darkness, and I was being very careful not to knock over anything in the cupboard. I didn't know what this thing was capable of. The sound of wet stomping grew closer as I held my breath.

Please don't see me. Please don't see me.

'S . . . ar . . . ah.'

A piercing shock ran through my body, a quiet gasp escaping my mouth.

That was my name. How did it know *my* name?

I heard it; I definitely heard it. Through the scratching and the gasping, I heard my name. I choked back tears, knowing if I made any more sounds, I would be dead.

It felt like an eternity inside the little cupboard – not knowing if I would ever see sunlight again, or if I would ever see Dad again. My mind flashed back to those happy memories I took for granted. How happy, warm and safe I felt in those moments. I would give anything to be there again, to be anywhere but here.

I snapped back to cold reality. The sound of the thing's hobbled trudge had subsided. Its gasping became quiet.

This was my opportunity right now to make it out with my life. It was now or never.

I placed my palm against the cupboard door and slowly pushed, taking care to avoid any creaking.

The darkness began to take shape as my eyes adjusted, just enough to make out the black-and-white tiles strewn with small inky footprints trailing through the kitchen.

I crawled out of the cupboard, making sure the thing was gone. I was a mess of paint, sweat and tears, but I wasn't giving up yet.

I took a deep breath and readied myself again into a runner's stance, mentally planning out the office route back to the elevator. Despite being in the other room, the thing's scratchy gasps knocked around in my brain.

On your marks.

I felt stupid for rationalising this wretched nightmare as a race to the finish line, but I couldn't deny the wave of confidence that washed over me.

Get set.

No matter how fast that thing thought it was, I *knew* I was faster. No way was I letting that stupid creature eat me.

Go.

'Sar . . . ah.'

My body flinched at the sound of my name. It was so clear; it sounded so close. In my mental preparation, I had drowned out the raspy, wheezing breaths that were still in the room with me. Whatever had said my name, it wasn't the thing stalking me. It was coming from behind me. It was coming from the wall.

'Sa . . . rah.'

That voice. I know that voice. It can't be.

I slowly turned my head. My widened eyes could scarcely make out the details of the dark shape in the middle of the wall, but everything slowly came into focus.

'. . . Dad?' The word escaped my mouth in a quiet whisper.

It was Dad, but it wasn't him.

My brain strained for details, barely recognising the patterns that resembled my dad. They weren't as I remembered. His face and body had been stretched and contorted, leaving in its place a distorted image of what was once my dad. I watched in horror as Dad continued to wheeze and choke for air as his thin body lay flat against the kitchen wall. I didn't know how to help him.

Dad groaned and choked as he peeled an arm away from the wall. I couldn't look away as the crooked arm unstuck itself and lurched towards me.

His voice was barely human, straining to form words.

'R . . . u . . . n.'

I felt fear take over. My heart beat out of my chest, until a horrific scream escaped my mouth, bouncing off the walls and piercing my own ears.

I turned around to face the kitchen door and watched as the thing stuck its distorted head through the doorframe. It had found me. A loud, pained screech accompanied it as it stumbled into the kitchen. I didn't have time to say goodbye to Dad as I sprinted towards the door, aiming for the small gap in between the thing's leg and the doorframe. It was just wide enough for me to dive through. I took my chance and jumped past the thing, crumpling onto the wall behind. My feet scrambled to find their position as I picked myself up off the floor.

The hallway ahead was empty. *I could make it.*

I got to my feet before my vision shifted from the hallway to the floor as my face collided with the carpet below. Something had grabbed my foot. I craned my neck to see the thing tightly wrapping its crooked arm around my leg.

'Get off! Get off me!'

The thing slowly pulled itself towards me, squeezing tighter around my leg until the pain became so immense, it felt as if my bones would crush under the weight.

I looked down at my leg. It was becoming thinner and thinner.

Crack.

Like a small twig that someone had accidentally stepped on, my leg snapped in two. The adrenaline coursing through me dulled my pain sensors, just enough for me to overcome the pain temporarily.

My leg was flat, a crooked remnant of what it once was, but thin enough that I could slip through the thing's grasp.

I scurried back and got to my feet, being very careful not to put any weight on my broken leg, knowing it could snap again at any given second. The slippery walls didn't help as I hobbled down the hallway.

The thing let out another screech that echoed through the office. I wanted to cover my ears, but with both hands keeping me upright, I didn't have a choice but to listen.

I approached the corner of the hallway, catching a glimpse of the long white corridor that awaited me. I looked behind me to see the thing had stopped chasing me and was lying motionless on the ground except for its head, watching my every move. I lost sight of it as I turned the corner, focusing on the corridor in front of me.

The pain started to become unbearable. I knew my body wasn't going to take much more.

It was eerily quiet, excluding the faint hum of the fluorescent light bulbs. The corridor seemed to stretch on forever. I glanced inside the offices as I stumbled past. They all seemed so ordinary, though I knew now this place was anything but.

Rip.

I paused for a moment. I couldn't tell if what I'd just heard was in my head. It didn't matter either way, nothing was stopping me from getting out of here. I glanced inside another office. *7.59 pm.* Had it really been that long? It was strange to think it was still the same day. A few hours ago, Dad had picked me up from school. Everything seemed so normal. But now, any sense of 'normal' was distant. My memory of Dad was replaced by the disfigured version in the kitchen. Hot tears began to stream down my face.

It didn't feel right to leave him behind.

Rip.

Was I a bad daughter? Should I have tried to save him? He told me to run because he knew it was my only chance to live. Even in his condition, Dad was still thinking about what was best for me. A pit slowly formed in my stomach knowing Dad was right behind me yet there was nothing I could do to save him.

'I'll come back for you, Dad, I promise.'

Rip.

Saying the words out loud made me feel a little better. I was getting out of here.

Rip.

I couldn't ignore that noise anymore, it was real. I scanned the space in front of me and behind me. There was nothing there, though I couldn't shake the feeling something was watching me.

Rip.

This time it was close. I heard it as clear as day.

I snapped my gaze to the stark white walls and searched the area.

There it was.

I winced at the sight of the little black flaps sticking out from the walls down the corridor. I quickened my pace into an awkward speed walk. My eyes widened in horror as the black spots grew larger, beginning to unstick themselves from the white walls, leaving large black silhouettes in their place.

The office slowly plunged into darkness as the white walls turned black, filling the corridor with countless demented, crooked things. Still running as fast as my damaged leg would let me, I let out a whimper as my hope turned into despair. They were behind me, they were in front of me, there was no chance of turning around now.

The closer I got to the end of the corridor the more of those things emerged from within the walls.

I was surrounded. My hand that was resting on the wall slipped as the monster underneath emerged, causing me to lose balance and land on my bad leg. The searing pain shot up through my body as my bones shattered. I crawled with all my strength as the things began to squeeze and tighten their crippled limbs around me.

As my body was being compressed from the inside out, I felt my arms and legs shrink.

My screams turned into raspy gasps for air.

The pain was too much, my vision blurred and then everything went black.

I felt myself stir awake.

I could hear birds chirping outside.

How long had I been asleep?

The memories of last night started to piece themselves together. It was hard to distinguish whether it was real or just one of the worst nightmares I've ever had.

I tried to blink away the blur from my eyes, but it didn't help.

I wanted to rub my eyes, but I couldn't reach them. My arms felt . . . stuck.

As hard as I tried, my arms wouldn't move.

I could feel myself starting to panic.

It was hard to breathe as my lungs strained for air.

'D . . . a . . . d.'

My voice felt foreign to me. All I could make out were faint gasps.

I could barely make out the sound of squeaking getting louder . . .

I tried to turn my head towards the sound, but it was useless. I was completely stuck.

Whoever it was, was getting close. The footsteps didn't sound like Dad's, but right now, I'd accept help from anyone.

It was hard to make out the figure standing in front of me. It was an adult, but they were at my eye-level.

Suddenly, that familiar smell hit me all over again.

It could only be described as a mix of strong cleaning chemicals and a smell that I couldn't quite place, but it reminded me of Grandma's funeral.

That smell. The more I thought about it, the more I could remember. Grandma always had that smell about her. I remembered trying to hug her, before she would push me away. Grandma always wanted a shower after work, but she could never quite get rid of that smell.

The figure bent down to grab something from their trolley and a cold sensation began to trickle though me.

'He . . . lp . . . me . . .' I tried to mouth to the person.

The figure didn't respond.

Coldness rose up my body and eventually covered my face.

The sound of a paint roller darted between my ears as the figure moved back and forth.

The roller covered my face and filled my vision with a blinding whiteness.

I couldn't move.

I couldn't see.

The sound of squeaking wheels began to subside.

Time passed. I couldn't tell if it had been minutes or hours. I'd lost track.

I heard the squeak of a door followed by the shuffling of footsteps.

Telephones rang.

Printers were printing.

Workers were working.

'Morning, everyone. It's a brand new day!'

EMAIL RECEIVED!

FROM: <CONTACT@████████.COM>

YOU WITNESSED AN ENCOUNTER. WE ARE ON THE RIGHT TRACK.

YOU CAN CALL ME FREEMAN; I WILL BE YOUR POINT OF CONTACT.

THE TEAM SENDS THEIR REGARDS FOR THROWING YOU IN THE DEEP END.

WE HAVE LIMITED TIME UNTIL THE ARC TRACKS US IN THEIR SYSTEM.

SEARCH THE ARCHIVES AND YOU WILL FIND YOUR ANSWERS.

ALL WE ASK IS YOU SHARE YOUR FINDINGS WITH US.

IN TURN, WE WILL PROVIDE SUPPORT FROM OUR END.

THE GEOGRAPHICAL SIGNATURE OF THIS LOG POINTS TO THE ARC HEADQUARTERS, ABOVE GROUND LEVEL. IT IS UNKNOWN IF THE RESIDENTS WERE AWARE OF THE ARC'S ACTIVITIES BELOW.

THIS WAS THE LAST KNOWN SIGHTING OF THE TARGET FOLLOWING THEIR ESCAPE FROM THE ARC.

KEEP YOURSELF GROUNDED, LOOK FOR CHANGES IN YOUR SURROUNDINGS.

HE MAY BE WATCHING.

ALEC THRIVES
FREEMAN

HAPPY BIRTHDAY

DATA CORRUPTION 89%
RECOVERING REMAINING DATA . . .

8 December 2022
Dear Diary,

I can't sleep tonight, I'm too excited!

Tomorrow's the big day. I'm finally gonna be an *adolescent*. It just sounds so *fancy*.

I wonder what being a teenager is like. Am I still going to like playing with my dolls?

Pfft, that's little kid stuff now.

Either way, I went shopping with Mum today and couldn't help but sneak a peek inside the shopping bag. She knows me better than I thought . . .

I guess I'll stick with my dolls a little longer. Who else is going to live in the pink hotel?

Oh, and I bet Hannah will be so jealous!

Dad's gonna pick us both up from school tomorrow for my birthday sleepover. I've got the whole night planned already. It's just us girls since Cameron chose to have his party last week. Something about some Battle Royale game night . . . *Whatever,* as long as he isn't here to do his twin big brother routine. I *hate* when he does that. I just *had* to be born five minutes after him and he'll never let me forget it.

I've been thinking about what I'll wish for this year. I know it's stupid. Blowing out a bunch of candles won't make all my dreams come true, but it's nice to pretend. There's just so much to see in this world, and I want to see it all. Mum always talks about wanting to go on a holiday and travel, but she never does.

Don't worry, Mum. I'll take you to Paris one day.

I know it's a while off, but I feel like there just isn't enough time to see it all. I mean, I'm already (almost) thirteen. My life is, like, literally half over.

That's why this year I'm going to wish that *I live forever.*

---

10 December 2022

LAST NIGHT WAS A MOVIE.

I'm pretty sure that was the first time I was awake to see the clock tick over to 3 am. Dad even came in and told us to be quiet! He was nice about it though.

Everything about yesterday was perfect. Just perfect.

Well . . . nearly perfect.

There was this weird moment when everyone was singing 'Happy Birthday'. I swear I could see someone through the kitchen window. He just stood there the entire song.

Maybe he was on his way home from work and wanted to see what the fuss was.

I dunno, it was just . . . weird.

---

14 May 2023

Here's a mental note to you, self. Next time you want to bring your dolls to school, DON'T.

God, that was so embarrassing. Even Hannah joined in with the other girls, all snickering and laughing. She's the one that told me to do it!

I know she had her dolls in her bag . . . I thought she was my friend. She's too smart to hang out with the mean girls. I miss the old Hannah. I miss hanging out at the library.

High school just sucks. It's not the same. Everyone likes to act so much older and *mature. Bleh.* Dumb. Everyone keeps treating me like a kid just because I'm the shortest in my grade. Whatever. I know they all go home and do the same stuff I do.

Bunch of fakers . . .

The day wasn't so bad after that. Mum and Dad were both working so G-ma picked me up for takeaway dinner. She asked me if I still wanted the toy with my meal . . . I said yes.

We talked about what happened at school (I think she went through the same stuff when she was my age). We talked for hours about everything.

She's always looking out for me. I really like that about her. I wish I could talk to Mum about stuff like this. G-ma thinks the reason we argue all the time is because we're so similar.

'If nobody died, it can still be fixed.' That's what G-ma said. It's been stuck in my head.

---

28 August 2023

Cameron was actually nice to me today. I wanted to write it down since it doesn't happen often, and I don't want to forget. His basketball game was cancelled because of the rain, so he stayed home with me instead, spending the afternoon building 'secret bases' like we used to.

Mum brought some snacks for us while we binged old Disney movies. *Kronk's New Groove* is still our favourite, that movie *never* gets old.

---

2 November 2023

I missed school today. While I was getting dressed, Mum and Dad were in the kitchen doing that totally not obvious (very obvious) 'loud whispering' thing.

They spotted me and smiled until I went back to my room. I didn't think much of it until we got to school. When Cameron got out of the car, Mum told me to stay.

I wasn't gonna argue with a day off.

I would've just spent lunchtime in the library anyway since Hannah's still hanging with those other girls.

The entire drive Mum kept asking me over and over, 'Are you feeling okay?'

I must have told her yes at least a thousand times.

I was glad to see Dr Jones was in today, she always gives me a treat after she's done her doctor stuff. They checked the usual like my height and weight and then another doctor took me to get some X-rays done.

That was new.

I definitely hadn't broken anything lately, so I thought it was weird they had to look at my bones. When I came back to Dr Jones's office, Mum was crying with her head in her hands. She didn't tell me what was wrong until we got home. Mum and Dad sat me down on the couch and told me.

'You've stopped growing.'

They didn't know why. I guess the doctors didn't have an answer either.

Dad thinks it's puberty doing its thing, but I've never seen Mum that upset.

Before bed, I checked my height chart etched into the doorframe. I could see Cameron was still updating his every few weeks – he's definitely going through a growth spurt. I stepped next to mine and etched it with a pencil.

Yep, they were right.

I've stopped growing.

---

9 December 2023

Here we are again, Diary. Fourteen today. Today was my special day but honestly, it was the last thing on my mind.

It's been over a month of compulsively checking my height chart three times a day. My family are known for being pretty tall. Cameron started his growth spurt as soon as he hit double digits!

I might just be the odd one out.

Whatever it is, it's not all bad. Everyone at school has started getting acne and even Cameron's voice is starting to crack. Guess being born five minutes earlier isn't all that it's cracked up to be, is it Cameron?!

Oh! I also have good news and bad news.

The bad news is I didn't have any friends over for my birthday this year.

The good news, though. You remember Hannah, Diary? She talked to me today. It's been months, but she came by the old hangout spot at lunch to say Happy

Birthday. She looks so different now, but I could see the old Hannah still in there. I asked her to come over tonight but . . . she's going to snooty Emily's house to make videos. *Whatever.*

---

27 December 2023

Something weird happened today. Cameron and I were playing with our new rollerskates that we got for Christmas. I'm still getting used to them, and well, I fell over.

I hit the ground hard and broke my arm.

Well, I thought I did. That's the weird part. It didn't hurt at all.

Cameron looked horrified. I didn't even realise my arm was twisted backwards until he pointed it out.

I didn't feel a thing, so I just . . . pushed it back into place. There was a loud crunch, and it was good as new. Cameron threw up as I stood there trying to wrap my head around what had happened. He wiped his mouth and just stared at me wide-eyed and petrified.

He told me not to tell anyone, not even Mum and Dad. It's hard to keep this bottled up, so I'm only telling you, Diary. I can't let anyone find you.

---

12 January 2024

It's been a few weeks since it happened. I've been thinking about it a lot. Something is very wrong with me, isn't there? Maybe it's a good thing?

Could it be that I'm a superhero? (A very, very short superhero.)

'With great power comes great responsibility' and all that.

I think I need to do some tests and explore the extent of my true powers. I'll write them down as evidence, just for you, Diary <3

HAMMER TEST – 13 January 2024 2.03 pm

RESULTS: 3 fingers broken. Healed almost instantly.

SCISSOR TEST – 18 January 2024 6.48 pm

RESULTS: Cut off pinkie toe with scissors. No pain besides a slight pinch. Observed pinkie toe regrowth in 15 seconds.

CAR TEST – 22 January 2024 4.24 pm

RESULTS:

---

22 January 2024

It's all my fault, I should've taken the blame. I needed Cameron's help for the third test. I wanted him to hit me with our car, but Dad caught us. Cameron in the driver's seat and me in the middle of the road. Dad was furious. I wanted to say something, but Cameron gave me *that look.* I can still hear Dad yelling at him. I don't know how he's going to explain it. How *do* you explain something like that?

---

2 February 2024

Photo Day at school. I guess being a secret superhero has its good parts. Not a single pimple on this beautiful face. Come to think of it, I can't even remember the last time I was *sick.* This cold spread through the school like wildfire last year – we even got a week or two off school. I thought I was just lucky, guess I know now.

The photographer was nice.

---

22 February 2024

Cameron came home today. He's been staying with our uncle for a month. Reading my diary about that day with the car, it seems like no time has passed. I still remember the look on Dad's face.

The guilt of not being able to tell anyone what really happened is still sitting like a rock in my stomach. I trust Cameron, though. He's my big brother, after all.

It was good to see him again. He gave me a smirk as he walked past me. I know that look.

He has something to tell me.

---

23 February 2024

Cameron snuck into my room after midnight. Dad *forbade* him from hanging out with me alone. He told me all about his month at Uncle Tom's. He'd been locked up in that house for too long.

Cameron is convinced he has powers too.

He showed me the small grazes on his arm, saying he's been doing his own tests. He's convinced that they're healing quicker than normal, but they just look like normal grazes to me.

Cameron wants us to do another test.

He wants to jump off a building.

'It's genetic, sis,' he kept telling me. 'We're twins. If you have it, then it only makes sense I do too.'

I think he's seen too many movies. Flight-or-fight response isn't going to make his powers kick in, I don't think it works like that.

Or at least, I don't think it does. I'm not exactly sure how mine works either.

Either way, the look in his eyes told me he's already made up his mind. I'm gonna try my best to talk him out of this. If I tell Mum and Dad, they'll know about *my* powers, and I don't think they're ready for that conversation yet. I have to stop this.

---

23 February 2025

I went to visit you today, Cameron. I made sure to freshen up your flowers.

It's still hard to think about. A whole year without you.

That day just repeats itself in my head.

Mum doesn't like to talk about it, and I don't think Dad will ever fully recover. He moved out a while back and we don't hear from him much. I think I remind him too much of you.

I hate this stupid curse.

I feel like I'm . . . stuck in that moment, forever.

---

8 March 2025

I read through my diary today, wanting to remember you – and I noticed something.

It was that wish, wasn't it?

That stupid birthday wish.

That's why I'm like this.

Oh god, am I really going to live forever?

I'll never grow older; I'll never be able to move on.

I look in the mirror and see the same girl as that day.

Just . . . so stupid.

---

2 April 2025

Mum found out today. Her little girl will always be her little girl.

It's kinda sweet, in a weird way.

She tried her best to ignore the fact that I haven't aged a day in years.

But when your mum watches you fall down the stairs and break your neck only to get up and walk it off, it's hard to hide it.

Mum took me to the hospital, as every responsible parent would. I don't know what she expected the nurse to say when they examined me and found nothing.

I was in perfect condition, not even a scratch.

She lied about my age, even in her panicked state. She knew mentioning that would only make things more complicated.

They gave Mum some medicine and told her to get some sleep. I guess they thought she hallucinated the whole thing.

Poor Mum. I think I'll talk to her tonight. She deserves to know the whole story.

---

5 April 2025

Mum begged me not to tell Dad.

I only see Dad at Christmas, but in his mind, I'm just a late bloomer. I wonder how long he'll keep that up.

After our talk, Mum gave me a hug and then we both cried.

She knows I'm scared, and I know she is too.

I know, at least for now, my secret is safe with her.

---

30 July 2025

I guess I'm homeschooled now. I think it's for the best because people were starting to ask questions. I don't mind, it's not like I was popular or anything. The handful of friends I had think I'm going to a prestigious private school; I thought I'd leave them on a positive note.

For a while it will be just Mum and me.

I'm gonna try to enjoy it for what it is.

Who knows how long we have left together.

---

28 June 2043

Hi Diary, it's been a while. Nearly twenty years, actually.

I wish I had time to write down everything that's happened while I've been gone, but I think those memories will be just for me. I'm happy I had that time with Mum. We both knew it was going to happen eventually.

She went peacefully.

The hospital took good care of her in the last few years. Seeing Mum bedridden was hard, but I stayed by her side as often as I could. I needed to be strong for her.

She brushed my hair, called me her sweet little girl and then . . . she was gone.

---

29 July 2043

Living with G-ma has been my safe space. It takes me back to those days before all this mess. Dementia has been really catching up with her in her old age. She still sees me as the same granddaughter I've always been and doesn't even bat an eye. G-ma accepts me for who I am, and I will always love her for that, even if she doesn't know any better. Every once in a while, she'll ask what time Mum is coming to pick me up. I just remind her that I'm sleeping over for the night, and the cycle starts again.

---

10 November 2044

I went to the park today.

I made a friend. (If you could call him that.) I'm old enough to be his mother, but to him, I was just a girl from another school.

We talked about life and our problems. I envied him.

I wish my biggest stress was getting homework done. He really was a bright kid, not that I was surprised. It all made sense once his mother came over to take him home.

It was Hannah.

It'd been decades since I'd seen her. She looked so grown up. I wish I could say the same for me.

I could tell she knew who I was – the look on her face said it all. Seeing your old best friend from twenty years ago looking exactly how you left her would be hard to process.

And then she called my name.

I said that was my mother. It was the best lie I could think of in the moment. She looked a little sad when I spoke about my mum. I suppose she feels guilty about how we left things. We spoke for a while and she listened to my fake story about the life I always wanted.

She introduced me to her kid, his name was Joel. Then they were gone.

Maybe in another life, Hannah and I could've become friends again and raised kids together.

I'd have liked that.

---

9 December 2044

Thirteen again today, Diary. Well, if we're getting *technical*, today I turned thirty-five.

Birthdays don't mean much to me anymore. Nobody remembers but me.

Mum's dead.

Cameron's dead.

Dad's missing.

G-Ma can't remember what year it is . . .

This is what I wished for, after all. I got what I wanted.

Guess I better make the most of it since I'm going to be here a while.

---

17 April 2046

Hi, Mum, this entry is just for you.

I finally made it, your final stop. I'm glad I could do this one last thing for you.

I got my wish, so I think it's only fair that you got yours too.

It's surprisingly easy to board a plane when you're a kid. Just turn on the waterworks and show them your ticket.

So I took you with me, spreading a little part of you all over the world.

You did it, Mum, you travelled the world.

Shibuya, Spain, Los Angeles, Chile and now, we've reached our final destination: Paris.

I'm going to rest up tonight before heading out tomorrow. You and I are going to the top of the Eiffel Tower. I'm sure it's got quite the view.

I think I'll leave the last of you up there with a view to last an eternity. I'm a little jealous. It'll be bittersweet to say our final goodbye, but at least we'll go out with a bang.

I'll head home after that and visit G-ma. She's in one of those special villages for patients with dementia. She loves it there.

I've got her house all to myself even after she passes. I found her will while cleaning the place up.

Even now she's looking out for her little granddaughter.

We've got a big day tomorrow, Mum. We better get some sleep.

I love you.

---

5 September 2052

Funeral services were held for George Knight on 2 September.

Dedicated husband. Loved and remembered by his three daughters and two grandchildren. George will be dearly missed.

It was Dad. I found his obituary online.

He was the last one. The last of my living relatives.

I'm not angry about Dad leaving and starting a new life. If I had the chance, I can't say I wouldn't have done the same. I get it. Having an immortal daughter and a son who jumped off a building, thinking he's a superhero, aren't things anyone would consider when deciding to have kids.

I'm sorry I couldn't be the daughter you wanted, Dad.

I hope you were happy, with or without me.

---

3 June 2062

Hi Diary, I got a present for you today.

I picked up one of those new neural link gadgets. Now all I have to do is think about something and the brain scanner writes it down for me! Kind of like a brain diary. Call me old-fashioned but I preferred the ol' pen and paper. It added a certain quality.

You're getting old too, Diary. You've been with me for over fifty years now. Guess this makes you immortal too. Just the two of us together till the end of eternity.

---

9 December 2070

Happy Birthday to me.

Happy Birthday to me.

Everyone I ever loved is dead,

Happy Birthday.

To me.

---

28 December 2076

The stars were beautiful from the backyard. I bet you're all up there, looking down on me, laughing.

It's a pretty funny joke.

'Be careful what you wish for!'

G-ma told me that once . . . should've listened to her.

Oh well.

I bet this is why they don't let kids get tattoos, or vote, or make any lasting decisions that may come back to haunt them.

Well, in most cases, till they die. But not me. I wanted to live forever.

---

29 March 2084

What do you do with spare body parts? Asking for a friend.

I got bored and now I've got so many piling up that I don't know what to do with them.

Donating them to science is a good bet, though I think they'd be curious how I came to collect several limbs belonging to a thirteen-year-old girl.

They'd phone some secret government agents who would lock me up in an underground facility and poke and prod at me till the end of my days, or theirs.

---

9 December 2109

For exactly one hundred years I have walked this earth.

One hundred long years.

The 'fun' died out half a century ago. Living forever isn't fun when nobody else is.

You never think about the end when you're at the beginning.

It's only when you're conscious of how much time is left that you stop to think that one day, everything, everything, *everything* eventually comes to an end.

I know how long is left.

It puts things in perspective. Everything I cared about was gone within a century.

Life was designed to end. That's what makes it special.

Every book has an ending, every song a final note.

And by wishing to live forever, I robbed myself of the one thing that made life . . . special.

Anyway, I better make some dinner. It's another day tomorrow.

---

19 August 2165

What do you do when you run out of things to *do*? What comes after you've read every book, taken up every hobby, watched every movie, heard every song? With no responsibilities and all the time in the world, eventually there comes a point where you've done everything.

Once it's finished, you can't experience it again. It becomes predictable.

The one truly unpredictable thing in this world is humans.

They're surprisingly messy and curious. You never know what they're going to do next.

I miss that; I miss people. I might try to make a friend.

---

2 September 2274

I quickly found that making friends wasn't an option. People begin to ask questions after a few years. It's more fun to watch from a distance anyway.

The internet is crazy, isn't it? A permanent record for humanity.

I watched my friend as he grew up, fell in love, got married, had kids, settled down, played golf on weekends, retired and died.

Then came his offspring. They grew up, fell in love, got married, had kids, settled down, played video games on weekends, retired and died.

Then came their offspring. She grew up, fell in love, got married, had kids, settled down, collected antiques on weekends, retired and died.

Then came her offspring. He grew up, fell in love, got married, had kids, settled down, went hiking on weekends, retired and died.

You get the picture.

I guess after a while, even humans become predictable too.

---

22 December 2483
It's been a few hours since the emergency broadcast.

Funny how a few words can send the entire world into chaos.

In three years, humanity will be extinct.

A supergiant asteroid collided with a star, altering its path directly towards Earth.

It's only a matter of time before humanity begins to collapse. I've lived through enough history to know that civilisation will be over long before the asteroid hits.

---

17 August 2485
I don't see many people anymore.

Last year was calm. Humans continued their day-to-day routines, hoping the brilliant scientists would figure it out and save the day.

It didn't work out quite that way. There was one shot and humanity missed it.

The dread slowly crept in as humans began to realise this really was the end.

Clean water was the first to go and soon it was everyone for themselves.

I'm not too fazed.

It hurts a little not having food and water for a few months, but I'll survive. It's the thing I do best.

But, for now, I think I'll explore what's left of Earth before that goes too.

I'm sure it looks pretty from way up in space.

Maybe soon I'll have my chance to see what that looks like.

---

6 December 2486

It's quiet.

I can't quite remember how long I've been walking, but I think I've found a nice spot to settle in and watch the end of the world.

We've got some time to talk, Diary. Let me tell you about my most peculiar day.

I met the strangest person.

He stood out to me since humans are scarce nowadays.

Even more peculiar, he was dressed like the old days, back when my family was around.

I can't quite recall their names anymore, but his clothes reminded me of them.

He wore a tan-checked suit and a bowler hat. He didn't smell very pleasant but that's to be expected by now. I wondered how this man was wearing clothes that haven't existed for five centuries.

I followed him for a while. He didn't seem to notice me. It was nice to see someone again.

But then this strange feeling washed over me. I felt like I knew this person.

Had I seen this man before?

When you've lived for nearly five hundred years, time starts to blend and blur.

The man then turned around to meet my gaze.

Even from a foot away, his face was hard to distinguish. All that could be perceived was a vague collection of facial features. He took off his bowler hat and nodded at me.

He raised his head once more, bringing a faraway memory to the surface. It felt so ancient yet so fresh in my mind.

I was taken back to the day when I made that terrible wish.

He was there. He was staring at me through the window.

I snapped back to reality and found myself standing alone in the desert. The man was gone.

For the first time in a very, very long time, I had questions.

Questions I knew were not going to be answered. I laid in the sand for a while after that.

What a strange individual.

---

7 December 2486

The asteroid is kind of beautiful up close.

For the past twenty-four hours, I've watched as it moved slowly towards the blue marble we call home. It's only a matter of time now.

The calm, blue skies are now a hellish-red, the air growing thicker and heavier by the hour.

At this point, all humans are extinct. They're not exactly built for such harsh climates.

Luckily for me, my skin heals fast enough for it to not melt from the heat. I'm the only living thing on Earth that gets to watch the end of the world.

I wonder where I'm headed next on my journey. Maybe I'll finally get to see the stars.

Or maybe I'll be lucky enough to die.

I guess we'll soon find out.

---

9 December 2486

The stars really are beautiful.

Although my lungs scream and gasp for oxygen every

waking moment (a side effect of my human anatomy), I can still appreciate the cold, infinite expanse of space.

I've thought about this moment for a while, it was always going to happen. The moment I would leave Earth behind.

To be honest, I'm a little jealous of all those beautiful shimmering stars. They too are mortal. They're born, shine brilliantly and then die. As all things should.

I . . . sorry, it gets quite hard to think without oxygen going to my brain. I think I'll rest for a while.

Oh, thank you for the reminder, Diary. I nearly forgot. Happy Birthday.

43,428 ADDITIONAL LOGS CORRUPTED . . .
END OF RECOVERED LOGS . . .

EMAIL RECEIVED!

FROM: <CONTACT@█████████.COM>

AN UNFORTUNATE END FOR THE GIRL.
SHE LIVED A THOUSAND LIVES SO FAR FROM HOME.
THERE IS NO TIME FOR REFLECTION. THE MISSION MUST CONTINUE.

IF YOU START TO FEEL LIGHT-HEADED, MAKE ATTEMPTS TO GROUND YOURSELF IN REALITY. LIGHT-HEADEDNESS IS A SYMPTOM.

IF THINGS SEEM DIFFERENT, THEY PROBABLY ARE. BE CONSCIOUS OF YOUR SURROUNDINGS. HE MAY BE NEARBY.

UPDATE: THE ARC ARE AWARE OF A PRESENCE IN THEIR SYSTEM.

KEEP LOOKING, THEY ARE ONTO US.

THE ARCHIVES CONTAIN THE INFORMATION WE ARE LOOKING FOR.

DO NOT FAIL US.

WE WILL PROVIDE SUPPORT FROM OUR END.

CHESTER VILA
FREEMAN

PLEASE DON'T GO

Slow cooker for dinner, yuck.

I didn't dare complain about it to Mum.

I watched from the couch as Mum let out a long sigh and hung her apron on the cupboard door.

'Kids, get your dinner,' she mumbled from the kitchen, making a ruckus with the utensils. 'Kids! Now! Dinner's ready!' Mum's yell echoed through the house. I shot up out of my seat, eager to avoid her wrath.

The upstairs bedroom door squeaked open. 'Coming! Don't need to yell!' Amy barked, stomping her way down the stairs.

Mum shot Amy a judging eye before settling back into her familiar Mum persona.

'I'm sorry for yelling . . . my darlings,' Mum exhaled. 'Please come and eat your dinner.'

Amy gave a smart look before grabbing a plate of food. I could almost see the steam coming off Mum's head.

Dad placed his plate on the bench, whispering something in Mum's ear. I could see tears fill in the corner of her eyes.

'It's so hard, Ted, why is she like this? What happened to our little girl?'

'She's growing up, babe. You were a teenager once too, remember?'

I pretended not to hear and grabbed my plate, quickly shuffling into the living room. It's been years since we used the dining table for dinner. I preferred to eat in front of the TV in silence anyway – it's less awkward than having to make small talk with a mouth full of food.

Not that we *wanted* to talk to each other.

It's still heated between all of us. Not even ten minutes ago, I was arguing with Dad about screen time, Mum was yelling at Amy about curfew and now we're all in a sour mood.

I guess we're all as stubborn as each other. We are related, after all.

I joined Amy on the couch. She kept her eyes firmly glued to the TV as I walked past.

'You made Mum cry,' I said, furrowing my eyebrows.

'You made Dad yell,' she replied, shrugging.

She had a point. I *hate* when she has a point. She does this big sister role a little too well.

Mum and Dad joined us on the couch a few minutes later with forced smiles. We all sat together as one big 'happy' family.

Dad swiped the remote from Amy's lap and flicked through the channels until he found the news. I should've known, it's nearly 6 pm. Mum and Dad *always* watch the news. It's not all bad though. They let us watch *The Simpsons* afterwards.

Mum was staring daggers at me from across the couch. I quickly stabbed some peas with my fork and shoved them in my mouth, managing an awkward half-smile.

She didn't look impressed (she hates when we don't like her home-cooked meals). Mum's a great cook, but I just can't *stand* slow cooker dinners. One night a week, Mum raids the pantry and throws whatever she finds into a big pot. Oh goody.

Mum shifted her eyes over to Amy.

'Mmm! So good!' I say in Amy's direction. She's too busy on her phone to notice Mum eyeing her down.

Mum let out an obvious fake cough to get Amy's attention.

Amy glanced up from her phone to see Mum's look of disapproval. She filled her fork with food, which seemed to make Mum happy enough to go back to eating her own dinner. At least it was quiet now. I could watch TV in peace.

'Coming up next,' the woman on the screen blared, 'a new development in a string of mysterious deaths as another young victim has been found. More details after the br–'

The TV suddenly went black. I whipped around to see Dad's hand still on the remote.

'So . . . how was school?' Dad asked.

'I was watching that,' I replied.

'Not anymore, you're not. You don't need to hear about that,' Dad insisted.

'Why not, it's public television,' Amy cut in.

'Yeah, Dad, and I thought this was part of my screen time, you can't just turn –'

'Yes, I can!' Dad cut me off, hiding the remote under his thigh. 'If I say you're not watching it, then you're not watching!'

'Wow, Dad, how do you expect him to follow the rules when you can't,' Amy snapped.

Mum gasped.

'You do *not* talk to your father like that! Go to your room!' Mum yelled.

'I –'

'No talking. Bedroom. Now,' Mum snapped. She was past the point of trying to be nice.

Amy picked up her plate and stormed into the kitchen, loudly dropping it in the sink before stomping back upstairs. Dad let out a big, tired sigh, rubbing his eyes with two fingers.

'James, please don't side against me like that. I wasn't trying to –' He was stumbling over his words. 'I was just trying to protect you, mate. I don't want you having nightmares again.'

I knew what he meant, but I don't like being babied. I'm twelve now, I can handle it.

We continued eating in silence until Mum eventually grabbed her and dad's empty plates and took them into the kitchen.

I pushed the peas around with my fork. My appetite was gone. I looked up and it seemed like Dad wanted to talk to me, but we just sat together awkwardly until I broke the ice. I couldn't bear the tension any longer.

'You just treat me like a little kid all the time, it's annoying! I've seen way worse than the *news*.'

Dad let out a groan before getting up from the couch.

'Finish your dinner then get straight to bed. You've got school in the morning.'

I looked back at my plate filled with food. I was gonna be here a while.

Time had passed and I wasn't any closer to finishing. It had gone cold, but knowing Mum, she wasn't going to let me leave until my plate was spotless. It's always a waiting game on slow cooker night to see who'll give in first. But tonight, I'll wait all night if I have to. Mum needs to accept that I am *not* eating my vegetables.

Dad poked his head back into the living room.

'Mum and I are going upstairs for a bit. Once you're done, please wash up and get ready for bed.'

I looked at him and then back down at my plate, nodding.

'And while you're down here, I want you to have a good, long think about your behaviour tonight. You've made your Mum and me pretty upset.'

I didn't know what to say, so I didn't say anything. Dad's head disappeared around the corner and I was all by myself. Just me, cold vegetables and the sweet, sweet TV.

I dug the remote out from the couch and switched it on, the room suddenly bursting with life as an ad's catchy music filled the space. I cautiously looked around to see if anyone noticed the noise, but I was in the clear.

I settled into the couch, leaving my plate on the floor, ready to enjoy some alone time with me, myself and some cartoons.

'Welcome back, you're joining us as we bring to light new details in a seemingly unrelated string of mysterious deaths that have left experts baffled. Viewer discretion is advised.'

Great, the news was still on. The reporter lady was still talking about that same story Dad didn't want me to listen to. He would *kill* me if he caught me watching this.

Then again, maybe this was my chance to prove to Dad how mature I was now, and that I could totally handle this kind of stuff. Dad let me play his grown-up video games sometimes, so it couldn't be too different than that. I took another cautious look at the doorway and then focused on the TV. The news lady was sitting at a desk with a picture of a taped off house behind her.

'A devastating incident has sent ripples through a small neighbourhood as another mysterious incident has claimed the life of a young boy.'

I started to feel a little uneasy.

'The quiet residential life of Smile Street was upended as a family discovered that their twelve-year-old son had suddenly died inside their home. We now go to an exclusive interview with the boy's parents.'

I gawked, wide-eyed at the screen. I hadn't even realised I'd buried my head into my legs to hide from it. I just needed to watch a little more until the cartoons were on.

I can do this.

The kid's parents were standing outside the house with red, puffy eyes, looking vacantly at the camera.

'We don't really know what happened. We heard him playing in the bathroom, talking to himself. I went in and he was on the floor with a bloody nose, shouting nonsensical things, and then . . . he stopped moving. The ambulance came, but by then it was too late.'

The boy's mum covered her face before falling into her husband's arms. The story then cut back to the news reporter.

I snapped back to reality and readjusted my horrified face. The hairs on the back of my neck were standing up, and I felt a little shaky. They didn't live too far from us. What if it was a deadly virus that was spreading? What if I was next?

My mind was racing with possibilities of what could have happened to that kid. Maybe Dad was right, I think I might have nightmares tonight, after all. I tried to calm my nerves with the breathing exercises Mum had taught me.

'The events on Smile Street were similar to those that occurred seven months ago in a nearby neighbourhood, where a young girl collapsed at her birthday party with the same injury. After an intensive investigation, paramedics could not find an explanation for her sudden demise.

'At this time, police refused t . . . any detai . . . the investigation.'

The reporter was interrupted as the screen flickered through grainy static.

'Stupid old TV,' I muttered. Our normal TV was getting repaired, so we were stuck with Grandma's ancient one till ours was fixed.

It was hard to make out the words as the reception grew worse and the reporter slowly disappeared into static. I grabbed the remote and flicked through the channels. Nothing. Every channel was replaced with loud, white noise. Rolling my eyes, I crawled towards the television. I reached behind it and fiddled with the antenna (I'd seen Dad do it a few times but I wasn't exactly sure *what* he did).

The living room went quiet as the loud static disappeared. I crawled back in front of the TV and looked at the screen. The news station was back but it was different. The reporter had changed. There was now a man at the desk sitting completely still.

It was deafeningly quiet as I focused on the TV. Why wasn't the man on the screen saying anything? Did he know they were on air?

I sat still. At least thirty seconds must've passed and yet the man on screen didn't move or say a word. He was completely motionless.

I felt unnerved as the man stared at the camera. It felt like he was looking at *me*.

My back was starting to ache from sitting on the floor, so I turned around to go sit on the couch. When I looked at the TV again, the man had moved. He was standing in front of the news desk still staring at the camera.

A wave of dread washed over my body.

Something wasn't right.

'Mum? Dad?' I called out, my voice trembling. I refused to break my line of sight with the man on the screen.

They must have heard me, but there was no answer.

I quickly picked up the remote and started flipping through the channels. The TV briefly flickered before showing the same man standing in front of the same desk. I rapidly pushed the button, flipping through at least twenty different channels, yet the man continued to stand there, motionless.

I didn't know what to do. I wanted to run upstairs and tell Mum and Dad, but then they would know that I'd disobeyed them. I didn't know which was worse, going up there or staying down here. It could just be a prank; I remembered Dad telling me once some prankster hijacked the airwaves back in the eighties to try to scare people. Maybe he was just doing it again.

It was getting hard to focus after staring at the same thing for what now felt like forever. I couldn't tell if it was my mind playing tricks or if the man was moving towards the camera. I got off the couch and moved closer to the TV. There was a slight hum coming from it. I didn't think it usually did that, and the noise was getting louder. I squinted at the pixels up close. The man was definitely moving closer – very, very slowly.

JAMES...

Against the hum of the TV, I could faintly hear what I thought were words. I pressed my ear against the TV speaker.

JAMES...

My blood ran cold. My heart was thumping out of my chest. I jolted backward and looked at the TV. The man was standing very close to the screen. His face was hard to make out even though he was only a few centimetres away. I couldn't tell if his face looked blurry or if it was just the old TV, but it was only partially visible from underneath his bowler hat. My breath was racing as I stared at the screen. The humming stopped.

JAMES

My name boomed out of the speakers before the TV switched itself off. I screamed as I tore out of the living room as fast as I could.

'Mum! Dad! Where are you?!'

The house was pitch-black except for the hallway light.

'Hello? Why are you all ignoring me?!' I shouted as I sprinted up the stairs on all fours. The light was shining underneath the door to my parents' room. It wasn't normal for them to be so quiet; it was only just after 6 pm and they surely must still be talking about earlier. I gripped the handle and creaked open the door.

'Mum? Dad? Are you in here?'

I scanned the dimly lit room and noticed Dad standing in the corner facing the wall.

'Dad! Dad, thank god you're here.'

I let out a nervous sigh of relief as I ran over, wrapping both arms around Dad's waist from behind.

'Dad, I'm sorry, I should've listened. I watched the thing you told me not to and now there's a creepy man on TV and I just really need you right now.'

I held Dad as tight as I could. I felt safe knowing he was here. Maybe I wasn't as grown-up as I thought.

I noticed Dad wasn't hugging me back. He just continued to stare straight ahead at the corner of the room in silence. *Is he that mad at me?*

I felt my hands start to slip lower and lower around Dad's waist. I thought that my arms were slowly falling, but Dad was *rising*. I looked down and realised Dad's feet weren't touching the ground. My eyes widened as I tried to comprehend what was happening. Dad was *floating*.

'Dad?! Dad, why aren't you touching the ground?!'

I started to panic, desperately pulling at Dad to try to turn him around. But even with all my strength, he wasn't budging an inch.

'What is happening? Please just look at me!'

No matter how hard I tried, Dad wouldn't budge. I could feel hot tears form. What felt like a safe space had completely warped into something out of my nightmares. Dad's body started to float higher and higher off the ground. In a few seconds, his head would touch the ceiling.

'Why are you doing this? I'm sorry. Please tell me you forgive me.'

I held tightly onto Dad's legs, using all my weight to bring him back down to the ground. It wasn't enough, but for the moment, he seemed to have stopped moving. Nothing could ever make me let go.

'I should have listened, I'm so sorry. I'm sorry. I'm sorry. I'm sorry.'

Dad didn't respond, and I buried my head against his back. I looked up to see him still motionless, looking at the wall. Scanning the room, nothing else looked out of the ordinary except . . .

'Mum! No!'

Through the bathroom door, I could see the lower half of Mum's body, her legs dangling in the air. She was floating too. I detached from Dad and ran over to Mum, desperately trying to pull her down to the ground as well. Just like with Dad, my body weight could stop her from getting any higher, but only just. Mum's face was visible in the bathroom mirror, but she was void of any emotion and her eyes were glazed over with a white tint. She looked like Mum, but not the Mum I knew. As I looked back through the doorway into the bedroom, I saw that Dad had begun floating higher and higher. I couldn't stop them both from floating away. I let go and sprinted back to Dad. The bedroom was silent except for my own screams of dread. I didn't know what to do.

I could see Dad's upper half as I passed back through the doorway. His head was gone. It had phased through the ceiling and disappeared. I desperately clung back onto Dad's waist, but it was no use, his head wasn't coming back down. I turned to see Mum continuing to float away in the bathroom.

I couldn't save them both. I wasn't strong enough.

I dropped to the ground, feeling completely powerless.

This wasn't how it was supposed to end. I didn't want my last memory to be of us spending the evening at each other's throats.

I should have listened to Dad. I should have eaten my vegetables. Maybe none of this would've happened if I had.

'Please don't leave me,' I whimpered into the silence.

I looked up and saw the rest of Dad's body disappear

through the ceiling. The bathroom was already empty. They were gone and I was all alone.

I pulled myself off the floor and wiped the tears from my face, thinking. They were gone from the house, but I might be able to see them from outside. I needed to find out where they were going.

I dashed downstairs and threw open the front door. The cold had arrived with the darkness of night-time. It was hard to make out but there were two faint silhouettes above the house. It was Mum and Dad rising into the sky. I clasped my hands around my mouth and yelled at the top of my lungs.

'Mum! Dad! Where are you going?!' It was no use, they were unresponsive. All I could do was watch as my parents floated away into the cold night air. My eyes slowly adjusted to the darkness and that's when I noticed that they weren't the only ones. Above all the houses in the neighbourhood, silent frozen silhouettes drifted into the sky. Entire families afloat into the sky without a sound. Why was I being left behind? I wasn't sure yet which fate was worse: left down here on the ground or unknowingly floating into the void with my family.

My family . . .

'Amy!'

In the chaos, I'd forgotten that Amy was still (I hoped) in the house. I pushed the front door open and rushed upstairs to Amy's room. Her door was slightly ajar. In between the dread and confusion of this night, I felt a wave of relief upon seeing Amy still in her room. But whatever was happening, it had got to Amy as well. She was floating a metre or two above her bed, her blanket still draped over her body. All the arguments we'd had, all the yelling and bickering, none of it mattered anymore. At this moment,

I was just happy to see her. I walked over to her bed to get a look at her face – she had the same glazed-over white eyes as Mum and Dad. Blinking back tears, I leant over her hovering body and gave her a hug.

'Hey, sis, thanks for sticking up for me tonight. Dad gets so mad when we work together, doesn't he?' I let out a small, teary chuckle.

'I don't know where Mum and Dad are going, but I hope you can stay here with me. I don't wanna be all alone tonight – I think it's another nightmare-night.'

A little part of me hoped Amy would smile back at me. A nod, a look, anything.

A few minutes had passed, and Amy still hadn't floated away. In fact, her body had moved back down to the bed. She wasn't nearly as heavy as Mum and Dad, or maybe I was strong enough to hold her back. For the moment, she was going to stay with me. It made me feel a little better. I pulled myself off Amy and stood back, taking Amy's hand in mine. It only took a little pull for me to drag her out of bed. It was bewildering to watch Amy's body gracefully move and twirl in the air as she floated, as if she were in outer space. I gripped her hand tightly, making sure I wouldn't accidently let go as I led Amy out of her room. It was still dark but I knew the way downstairs, and I took extra care to make sure Amy didn't hit her feet against the family photos along the wall.

The kitchen light hummed as I switched it on. I squinted against the brightness, pulling a chair and fitting Amy's body onto it. It was a little tricky with her limbs flying in all directions, but between the two of us we made it work. I needed to make sure she wasn't going to fly away from me. Once she was seated, I turned my attention to the kitchen drawers. There was something I needed.

'I don't know if you can hear me in there, Amy,' I said, 'but I really miss Mum and Dad.'

I looked back at Amy to check for a response. She was silently sitting in her chair. I began rummaging through the drawers . . . it had to be in here somewhere.

'I know that we don't always get along. There's been more times we've wanted to kill each other than there has been us just hanging out. But I'm glad you're here with me now.'

There, found it. I took it out of the drawer and carried it over to Amy, who was still floating in her seat. I kneeled next to her and raised her leg, looking into her glazed-over eyes.

'This way, I'll never let you go. It's just you and me noW.'

I took the riBBon and gently tied a double-knot around her ankle. As I moved the chair out from under Amy, she sl0wly floated up towards the ceiling. I grabbed the other end of the ribbon and tied it around my wrist. There was a gEntle tug as the ribbon reached its end and Amy fLoated above me.

'C'm0n, Amy, let's go watch some TV. I think cartoons are on.'

As wE# Dsoed oveR 7o th3 LIvi#★$ NNF★$# GHN@#F(WHVB$IBGIEWKGNH(VR

""H$#&FH(HD@#)JF)#N@

NU(#@HF&G $LN@M_DK+!I(UF#JI) @#$JGJ(J(★H9H

ONF(★#F#G$ L@)BK$#JG_!)HH&★GB★$G

DATA CORRUPTED
PLEASE CONTACT ADMINISTRATION

EMAIL RECEIVED!

FROM: <CONTACT@[redacted].COM>

THESE ENTRIES CONFLICT WITH OUR INTERNAL REPORTS.

THEY DO NOT MATCH OUR REALITY.

THIS IS A RECURRING PATTERN WITHIN THE ARCHIVES.

THE INDIVIDUAL PLAYS A PART IN THIS DISCREPANCY.

THE INDIVIDUAL ON TELEVISION IS OUR TARGET.

THE INDIVIDUAL IS CAPABLE OF FAR MORE THAN YOU THINK.

THE INDIVIDUAL IS NOT TO BE UNDERESTIMATED.

CONTINUE SEARCHING THE ARCHIVES.

WE HAVE INFILTRATED THE ANOMALY RESTRICTION COMMITTEE.

I CAN NOT LET THIS OPPORTUNITY GO TO WASTE.

CAVILS THREE,
FREEMAN

FLAT GRANNY

'Now remember, kids, Granny and Grumps are getting old. Granny's back isn't what it used to be, so we can't just jump on her as soon as we get in the door,' Mum said, craning her neck over the back seat.

I shoved my game back into my bag and heaved it over my shoulder, stretching my legs after the three-hour drive.

'Do we really have to stay here overnight?' I said, rolling my eyes. 'I can watch Lucy. I'm old enough to look after her.'

'Please don't make this harder than it needs to be, you know I have to work, Blake. The sitter was busy, and Granny and Grumps are so excited to see you again,' Mum replied, opening the door for Lucy to get out.

I let out an exaggerated sigh. Mum hates when I do that, but I really, really didn't want to come here.

I hate old people; they creep me out.

Granny and Grumps used to be fun when I was little, but now Granny always has this blank stare that weirds me out. It's like the lights are on but nobody's home.

As for Grumps, well, he's Grumpy. Mean, old, bitter Grumps.

'Blake, do you want to go knock and let them know we're here?' Mum asked.

I resisted another eye-roll as I dragged my feet over to the front door.

Granny and Grumps have lived in the middle of nowhere for as long as I can remember. This visit, the house looked worse than ever.

The gardens were overgrown, the front porch was cluttered with old furniture and dirty knick-knacks. It felt like a different world compared to our nice, normal house in our nice, normal neighbourhood. Mum had tried to get them to move closer when I was born, but Grumps refused, saying, 'I'll never sell this house!' Fine by me.

I hesitated at the door, knowing that as soon as I knocked it would be the start of the most boring twenty-four hours of my life. I looked behind me to see Mum swallowed in bags, helping Lucy out of the car.

Knock. Knock. Knock.

No answer. I looked back to Mum and gave a shrug.

'Knock louder, Blake, they're old.'

I turned back around and sighed, balling my hand into a fist.

Bang. Bang. Bang.

I could hear a faint thud from behind the door. I pressed my ear against it and tried to focus on listening.

'Wear . . . this.'

It was quiet and muffled but I definitely heard it. The door swung open with my ear still pressed against it, sending me tumbling to the ground. Two pairs of feet were suddenly inches from my face; one wearing dirty, old brown boots and the other wearing a pair of fluffy, yet slightly crusty, beige slippers.

The smell was terrible.

Old people.

I looked up to meet the gaze of dear old Granny and Grumps.

'Oh, hello, dearie,' Granny said with a smile, bearing her teeth. I picked myself up and dusted off my shorts.

'Granny, Grumps. It's . . . so good to see you,' I said sarcastically, knowing they wouldn't pick up on it. *Old people.*

'Don't be rude, Blake, they're happy to see you,' Mum said, nudging me in the back with her elbow.

I looked back at Granny. She looked the same but felt different.

Her eyes didn't match her smile and she seemed distant, like she was staring a thousand miles away. Grumps looked miserable as always. Such a grumpy guy.

'Granny!' Lucy shouted as she flew past me, wrapping her arms around Granny's legs.

'It's lovely to see you all, come on in. I've got the kettle on,' Granny said with a smile.

I followed them, stepping inside the old, dilapidated house. It reeked of stale air and dust. It looked like nothing had been touched in the past ten years.

'Granny! Where's my room? I have to set up all my toys!' Lucy beamed, holding a doll in each hand. She carried those things everywhere she went.

'Oh, honey, let me sort that out with Granny first, we'll need to set up a bed for you,' Mum replied, manoeuvring herself and the bags around all the boxes and furniture haphazardly strewn along the hallway.

Grumps motioned us into the kitchen where Granny was already opening the cupboards to fetch some mugs. She was wearing one of those hand-knitted shawls over her shoulders. It was the first time I'd seen her wearing something like that. It looked nice on her.

I watched as Granny struggled to reach the top shelf.

'Oh, Blake, be a dearie and help Granny fetch some mugs. Granny's back isn't what it used to be,' Granny said sweetly, before coughing violently.

I walked over to the cupboard and picked up a few mugs. A thick layer of grime covered the handles. I set them down on the counter before wiping my hand against my shorts.

'None for me, Blake, honey. Mum's gotta make a move, it's already past midday and I'm running late.'

Mum grabbed her handbag off the table before walking over to Granny, placing a hand on her shoulder and pecking her on the cheek.

'Ask Blake for help if you need a hand tidying up. This place is falling apart, Mum.'

Granny wrinkled her brows and tutted at Mum's comments. 'Don't worry, dearie, your father has it under control. Maybe these two munchkins can give Granny and Grumps some help with a little renovation.'

'Yay! Renovating!' Lucy squeaked. *She really does love playing house.*

'Okay, well, Lucy's bedtime is at seven. Blake can stay up for a couple more hours but no games after lights out,' instructed Mum, shooting me a look.

I replied with another eye-roll. *That's what she thinks.*

While Mum said goodbye to Grumps, I helped Lucy carry her bags into the second living room. She'd brought *so* many dolls, *no one* needed that many.

'Lucy, wait,' I whispered as Lucy whipped around. 'Does something seem . . . weird about Granny and Grumps? Like, weirder than usual?'

Lucy furrowed her eyebrows and shook her head. 'Don't be mean, they're just old people.'

I sighed as I followed Mum to the front door. We waved goodbye as she hopped back into the car. There went my last chance to escape; guess I really was stuck here for the next twenty-four hours.

'And . . . done,' I exclaimed, proud of the makeshift bedroom I'd helped make for Lucy. It looked like the only bedroom was upstairs, so we had to make do with a blow-up mattress in the second living room. Lucy was busy lining up all her dolls on the windowsill. I could hear her talking to them.

'Stacey, babe, this is such a great vacation, isn't it?' she said in a deep voice.

'Oh, Mark, you're so hot, this is the best vacation ever,' Lucy continued, in a slightly higher voice, making the dolls kiss repeatedly.

Where did she even *hear* this stuff?

The slight shuffling of feet against the floorboards pricked my ears as Granny stuck her head into the room.

'Hello, dearies, the telly's on in the other room if you'd like to join me.'

Lucy stayed behind, but I followed Granny into the living room. TV seemed like the only normal thing in this bizarre house.

It was a miserable little space, dimly lit by a TV the size of a microwave. I could only see the top of Grump's bald head as he sat in his recliner facing the television, watching what looked like a black-and-white re-run of an old sitcom. There was only one other chair in the room, which Granny was already slowly lowering herself into. It must have been a pretty cushy chair – she sank so far into the couch that I could barely see her face from the side.

'There's a spot on the rug for you, dearie. It's time for our soaps,' Granny said as she pointed to the stained, old carpet in the middle of the room. It was fraying at the edges and, even from here, looked very uncomfy.

'Granny, this carpet is uh . . . lumpy.'

Grumps quickly whipped his head around in my direction with an offended look.

'There's nothing . . . wrong with the rug. You kids these days always . . . complaining about . . . something,' Grumps huffed and wheezed as he dismissively waved his hand.

Granny bent over her chair and looked at me, or through me, I couldn't tell.

'Now, dearie, Grumps worked hard to fix this old house.' I couldn't focus on Granny's words without being distracted by her distant gaze. She still looked like she was a million miles away. She leant over a little closer, whispering in my ear, 'Rude boys will be punished.'

I felt a little uneasy looking back at Granny, her finger pressed against her lips. The tone of her voice was sweet, but her dead eyes gave her words an unsettling edge.

Grumps stayed motionless in his chair, unaware Granny was still talking to me. I sat on the uncomfortable rug, looking up at the old TV and readjusting every few seconds to ease the strain on my back. Every couple of minutes, I glanced back to see Granny staring at me, her finger still pressed against her lips. The excruciating awkwardness eventually got too much. I had to get out of there.

'I'm gonna go, uh, get something to drink. I'll be right back.'

I carefully avoided falling over the lumps and quickly shuffled out of the living room. Granny's stare was still boring into the back of my skull.

The atmosphere in the kitchen wasn't much different. Dirty plates and cups were stacked high in the sink, and the old cuckoo clock had been taken off the wall and carelessly shoved onto the counter, acting as extra bench space for even more cluttered mess.

I searched for the cleanest cup and turned on the tap. The pipes rattled and clanked as the water pressure slowly picked up, spitting out a yellowish liquid. I hoped it was water.

I took a small sip and gagged, tipping the rest back down the sink. It didn't taste anything like the water back home.

I surveyed the room, trying to avoid staring at the headache-inducing wallpaper for too long. It was made up of yellow and brown flowers that consumed the entire kitchen wall.

I was already feeling foggy and light-headed. The spaces without wallpaper were the doors to the living room, hallway and the basement . . . which was *locked*?

I looked closer and noticed not one, not two, but three separate locks on the basement door. Whatever was down there, Granny and Grumps wanted to keep it a secret. At this point, I didn't think I'd be surprised even if they were hiding dead bodies.

'Hello, dearie.'

I nearly jumped out of my skin as I turned around to see Granny standing directly behind me. I guess in her old age she'd forgotten about personal boundaries.

'Um, hi, Granny. I was just, uh, looking for the bathroom,' I quickly responded, trying to cover my obvious snooping.

She stared at me and slowly inched closer. I swiftly moved aside as she walked over to the basement door, pulling a set of keys out of her pocket.

'Basement has your curiosity, hmm, dearie? Don't fret, my dear, no dead bodies here, nothing of the sort. Granny isn't that adventurous,' Granny chuckled as she began unlocking each lock and placing them on the counter.

'Have a look for yourself, dearie. Don't mind the smell.'

Granny creaked the door open.

I gagged as the most wretched odour seeped out from the basement.

'Granny! What is that smell?!' I said, choking on my words.

Granny wasn't fazed. She smiled at me with her empty eyes, motioning with her bony finger for me to follow.

The old stairs creaked and moaned as I followed her down into the pitch-black basement. I took turns covering my nose and mouth, but the smell remained consistently unpleasant.

Granny pulled on a string hanging from the roof and the basement suddenly . . . stayed dark.

'Oh dear, must have blown a fuse. C'mon, dear, take my hand,' Granny said, grabbing my hand with her cold, wrinkled fingers.

'Actually, I should probably check on Lucy. She's –'

'She's fine, dearie. Grumps is with her,' she said as she led me deeper into the lightless basement.

'Curiosity killed the cat, so let's make sure it doesn't kill you,' she continued.

I couldn't see her face, but I could picture her lifeless eyes and mismatched grin perfectly. I collided with and tripped over knick-knacks and old furniture as Granny pulled me further into the basement.

'Ah, here we are, dearie.' Granny stopped in front of me, her shallow breathing the only sign of where she was in the room.

'Hold out your hand. Don't be shy, have a feel.' I felt myself tense as Granny pulled my arm forward. My hand connected with *something* that was hanging from the roof.

Whatever I was touching swung around as I pressed against it. I grabbed it with both hands and felt around with my thumbs. It felt rough and dried out, as if it had once been smooth but had been hanging for so long that it was now something else.

'What is it, Granny? It feels . . . old?' I asked.

'This is some of your Grump's latest handiwork. He's taken up a new hobby in skinning,' Granny replied joyfully.

I quickly recoiled my hand.

'S-skinning?! Like animals!?' I snapped.

Granny continued to softly chuckle to herself.

I felt sick to my stomach. I had just touched a dead animal, and I could already feel the germs seeping into my body. I held back vomit as I made a beeline towards the dimly lit stairs on the other side of the basement, leaving Granny behind in the darkness.

She didn't say a word as I rushed back up the stairs and into the kitchen. I turned the tap on and threw up into the sink. I vigorously scrubbed my hands under the water – the best I could do with no soap in sight.

I instinctively checked the basement door for Granny every few seconds. Something wasn't right, and not just because she was old. I guess the isolation of living with Grumps for nearly a decade had rotted her brain – she wasn't the Granny I remembered.

Thud.

Something in the house hit the ground, hard.

I brushed my wet hands against my shorts and walked back through the hallway to the other side of the house. Out of the corner of my eye I noticed the door to Lucy's make-shift bedroom. It was ajar and shadows flicked against it.

The floorboards creaked as I slowly moved towards the door, listening to the quiet mutterings in the other room.

'The columns . . . aren't . . . healthy. Do Grumps . . . a little favour.'

I didn't understand what Grumps was talking about. Perhaps it was just the train of thought of an old, senile man. I peeked around the corner to see . . . Lucy unconscious in Grumps' arms.

Was that the thud I heard before?

I mustered all my courage and ran into the room to confront Grumps.

'What did you do to Lucy?!' I yelled. There was no way she was sleeping. Only a few minutes ago I had seen Lucy playing with her dolls against the windowsill! Grumps had had a hand in whatever was going on.

'She . . . had a fall,' he muttered in between drawn breaths.

Something inside me refused to believe that Lucy had suddenly fallen and knocked herself out. She was a kid but she wasn't stupid.

'Oh, dearie,' I heard behind me.

I turned to see Granny slowly shuffling into the room. 'Don't be so hard on poor old Grumps; look around the room.'

I reluctantly observed the room and noticed some of Lucy's dolls perched on top of the tall dresser, surrounded by old kitchen appliances and junk.

'She obviously tried to climb up to fetch her dolls, dearie. She's just had a bit of a tumble,' explained Granny.

Is that possible? Could Lucy have accidentally knocked herself out reaching for her dolls?

'But just before I came in, I heard Grumps say, "the *columns* aren't healthy", whatever that means!' I yelled angrily. I was convinced they were lying.

'Oh goodness! It was just a simple misunderstanding, dearie. Grumps was calling Lucy his *blossom*. His *blossom* isn't healthy, just look at the poor girl, she's bleeding!' Granny explained.

I looked back down at Lucy and saw Grumps' hand on the side of her head, a small line of blood seeping out from between his fingers.

'But –'

'Not another word, dearie. Now isn't the time for your silly stories. Lucy needs some medicine.'

Granny wouldn't let me finish. I couldn't do anything but helplessly watch as Grumps carried Lucy out of the room. I followed close behind but was stopped at the door by Granny's bony hand in my face.

'Ah, ah, ah. *You* can stay downstairs. Lucy doesn't need you filling her head with your stupid stories.' Granny's tone felt pointed as her smile disappeared. She was visibly annoyed by my accusations.

I pulled a sour face and crossed my arms, turning my back to Granny and observing the mess in Lucy's room. I glanced back. Granny was gone.

I felt powerless to do anything. No one was listening to me.

I was going to need help.

I walked out of Lucy's room and into the hallway, peering upstairs to check for movement.

It looked empty, but I could hear muffled voices coming from a room upstairs.

I walked through to the kitchen, looking around for a landline to use – there was no way Granny and Grumps knew how to work a mobile.

I was stuck having to scan the eye-straining wallpaper for one of those old wall-mounted phones. Were my grandparents really this ancient?

The old, yellow telephone blended in well against the wallpaper, but it couldn't escape my keen eyesight. I picked up the phone and dialled Mum's number – she'd gone on so many business trips by now that I had it memorised.

The phone beeped loudly with each number I pressed, ending with a dial tone that nearly left me deaf. They must have turned up the volume.

Old people.

My teeth chattered as I waited for Mum to pick up on the other end. I periodically scanned the room behind me, hoping Granny and Grumps would stay too preoccupied upstairs to notice my call for help.

. . .

'Hello?'

Mum's voice brought the phone to life. A wave of relief washed over my entire body. I was getting out of here.

'Mum! It's Blake.'

'Blake? What are you calling me for?'

'Mum, just listen, I need you to –'

'Hang on, darl, slow down, I'm in a meeting. Let me just step out –'

The muffled conversation of Mum apologising to her boss played out over the phone. I felt bad for interrupting Mum at work, but this was more important. Her boss would understand.

While I listened closely, waiting for what felt like hours for Mum to leave the room, I heard something that seemed out of place. It didn't sound like it was coming from Mum's end of the line.

I could hear . . . breathing. It was faint, but the sound of someone taking quiet, deep breaths became noticeable.

A phone this old, the only other person who could join the call could be –

Oh no.

It was Granny, listening in to the call. She must have another landline upstairs.

She was listening.

'All right, Blake, honey, what's the big emergency?'

I froze, not knowing what to do. If I told Mum that Granny and Grumps were acting delusional, that would be the end of me. There's no way Mum would make it in time before I became another animal hanging in the basement.

'Blake? Hello?'

My mouth went dry, and the words I wanted to say wouldn't form. 'I . . . I –'

'Blake, what is it?'

The voice on the phone suddenly changed and I felt my blood run cold.

'Oh, hello, dearie.'

Granny had hijacked the conversation.

'Mum? Is everything all right? Blake's calling me and –'

'Don't worry your little head, dearie. Blake is standing next to me now. He was just wondering if he could stay up past his bedtime tonight.'

I couldn't believe it. Granny was lying to Mum without missing a beat. Was the 'senile old woman' all an act?

Granny's house wasn't safe anymore.

I was in danger.

'That's it?' Mum asked dismissively.

'That's it, dearie, sorry for the trouble.'

'Yes, that's fine, Mum. I'm really busy here, can you –'

'Don't worry, Granny will make sure he . . . has a good night's rest.'

'Okay, thank you, bye-bye.'

'Bye-bye now, dearie.'

The call ended; my mouth was still agape from what had just happened. The dial tone rang in my ear as I tried to process the fact that I had just blown my shot. I was stuck here until tomorrow.

I could hear the upstairs door slowly creak open.

I tried to steady my shaking hands as I hung up the phone. Someone was coming down the stairs. Dread started to consume me, and my mind ran wild with incomplete thoughts that overlapped into static noise.

'Blake, dearie. Granny isn't mad.'

Granny's words echoed down the hallway alongside the sound of her fluffy slippers shuffling on the stairs. My body, paralysed with fear, refused to move.

Every door from the kitchen led back to the hallway except for the basement, which was locked again. The key sat in Granny's pocket.

My eyes darted to the hallway as Granny's head appeared around the door. The rest of her body followed behind, her feet creaking against the wooden floorboards.

'Oh dear, now what are we going to do with you?' Granny asked, eyeing me up and down. She smelled of rotting meat and perfume as she brushed past me towards the sink, filling up a dirty glass with water. She looked up out the small window facing into the backyard.

'Hmm, the gardens could use some fertiliser,' Granny muttered to herself.

My body shook uncontrollably as I struggled to figure out who exactly this old lady was.

Granny turned back around to meet my stare, pushing a now full glass into my face. 'I suppose we should put you to some good use. Drink up, dearie.'

I grabbed the glass, despite every fibre of my being screaming at me not to. My survival instincts were telling me to obey so I would survive. Granny pushed up the bottom of the glass, making sure I finished every last drop of the water (if you could call it that). It was terrible and tasted of rust and medicine. I coughed and sputtered as I struggled to stomach the liquid. The fog returned, already starting to cloud my mind.

'What . . . did . . . you –'

The words struggled against my numbing tongue as the liquid sent a cold sensation through my limbs. My legs started to tremble as the weight of my body began to work against me. The blurred outline of Granny walked towards me, catching me midway to slow my descent to the ground.

'It's all right, dearie, give Granny a hug,' she whispered, grabbing my arms and wrapping them around her waist. She was deceptively thin. My hands easily clasped together behind her as I tried to hold myself up.

It struck me as odd since Granny looked round and plump from the front, yet her back was slim as if all her weight was on the front of her body. As my consciousness started to fade, I clung onto anything, wrapping a fist around Granny's knitted shawl and pulling it down with me. As my hand moved down her back, I felt it collide with bumps all the way down. Bile formed in my throat, and then everything faded to black.

'Blake, honey, wake up. You're gonna be late for school.'

I heard Mum's soothing voice while I lay comfortably underneath the warm blanket. A smile spread across my face as she gently tussled my hair between her fingers.

'Lucy's already downstairs having breakfast. You've slept through the whole afternoon.'

Snip.

'Do I have to go today? It's Saturday, and I've already finished all my homework.'

'Of course not, my darling. Stay in bed and sleep as long as you want.'

Snip.

'Also, Mum? Could you bring me some hot chocolate? The ones you make with the little marshmallows in it?'

'Yes, dearie.'

Snip.

Dearie?

Mum never called me that.

Mum came back a few seconds later with a mug in her hand. I could see pink and white marshmallows poking out on top. I wriggled myself upwards into a sitting position and held out both hands, ready to hold the drink. Mum stood at my side and held the mug just out of reach.

'Mum? The mug?'

Her smile started to widen, baring her teeth manically. Mum raised the mug directly above my head, never breaking eye contact.

'M-mum?'

She turned the mug upside down, sending the searing hot chocolate onto my head. I screamed in agony as the heat burned my flesh, melting the skin on my face. Mum threw the mug against the wall and jumped on top of me with her impossibly wide grin.

'Rude boys will be punished!'

I shot up off the floor, panting heavily as I tried to catch my breath. My singlet was completely soaked with sweat. I looked around the room to try to make sense of my surroundings. Dolls were stacked neatly along the windowsill.

It was dark outside. The air had a bitter chill to it that pinched at my arms and legs. It was freezing.

It was just a bad dream. Or was this a bad dream? I couldn't decide which scenario was worse. The memories of the afternoon slowly crawled back into my head: the skinned animals in the basement, Grumps carrying Lucy away, Granny lying to Mum on the phone. I was back in this nightmare.

My drenched clothes were an indication of how much fluid I'd lost. I was so thirsty.

I knew now that the water here couldn't be trusted. Whatever Granny and Grumps put in the water, it wasn't good.

The dolls on the windowsill reminded me that it had been hours since I'd last seen Lucy. I had to check on her. I needed to know if she was okay.

I creaked open the living room door and peeked out into the hallway. The house was completely still, everything was quiet.

Granny and Grumps must be asleep, I hoped. This was my chance.

I tiptoed into the hallway, carefully avoiding the clutter strewn over the floor and made my way towards the staircase, using the dim glow cast by the lamp next to the stairs as my only source of light. The family portraits along the staircase walls were a grim reminder of who Granny and Grumps once were. They looked happy. I couldn't help but crack a sad smile at the photo of Granny and Lucy together.

I remember that day like it was yesterday. Granny had taken Lucy and me to the beach. The sand was hot so Granny carried Lucy all the way down to the water just so she could splash around. She even bought ice-cream for us after.

What happened?

Everything was so different now.

I walked carefully to not wake Granny and Grumps, avoiding the broken step halfway up. One wrong slip and, well, I'd have an express ticket back down to the bottom.

I noticed a small mirror hanging between the portraits. I looked back at the person staring at me. It didn't look like me, I looked like a stranger.

My hair was gone.

Somebody had cut off all my hair. I ran my fingers over my buzzed head. How could I have not noticed that my hair was gone? It didn't even register that my hair would have also been drenched in sweat, sticking to my face.

They cut it all off.

Why?

The number of questions without answers began to quickly snowball. I didn't understand what was happening, any of it. I wanted to fall to my knees and cry, but now wasn't the time. I needed to find Lucy.

I spotted a door at the top of the stairs to the right. It was covered in locks and deadbolts, just like the basement. Lucy couldn't have been downstairs. She had to have been in the basement or behind that door. I jiggled the handle in case my luck had decided to turn.

No luck.

I let out a silent scream in frustration. I was so close yet so far. If only it were open, I could scoop Lucy into my arms and we could run away from this place. Something bad was going to happen soon and I had no intention of sticking around to find out what.

I pressed my ear against the rusty door and focused on the sounds.

'Mmm . . . uhhh.'

There was definitely someone inside. I had to get in there.

My mind flashed back to this afternoon when Granny opened the basement door. She kept the keys to the locks in her pocket. I could only hope they opened all the locks in the house. I didn't have any other choice. I had to find the key.

I turned around and looked towards the other end of the upstairs hallway where two doors sat. One of them had to be Granny and Grumps' room.

As I approached the doors, the sound of Grumps' snoring became increasingly clear. This was definitely their bedroom. I was going to get those keys, *I had to.*

The door was ajar enough that I was able to squeeze through without opening it further.

Grumps continued to snore away loudly in his bed surrounded by tall towers of unwashed clothes and rubbish.

How long had they been living like this? How did they live with this smell?

The carpet helped mask the sound of my footsteps as I crept to the other side of the room, the smell growing increasingly worse with each step closer to Granny's side of the bed. My foot felt wet as I stepped on a pile of clothes. I carefully lifted my foot up, running my finger along its sole and bringing my finger up to my face. The darkness made it hard to make out. I brought it up to my nose, my head recoiling against the putrid scent.

It was blood. Fresh blood.

I didn't have time to think about why Granny's clothes were drenched in blood, but I knew that they must have been recently worn. I covered my mouth with my clean hand as I squished my foot against the clothes, feeling around for the keys. I silently gagged and wretched as my foot became increasingly damp with each shallow stomp into Granny's clothes.

Ting.

There they were. The sound of keys clanging against each other. I didn't dare move as I patiently waited for Granny and Grumps to react. Grumps continued to snore away. I bent down and reached into the pocket and slowly pulled out the keys, making sure I gripped them tightly in my fist to avoid any more sounds.

Hard part over, nearly there.

With keys in hand, I retraced my steps back through the bedroom paying no mind to how dirty my feet were getting – there were bigger things to worry about. I squeezed back through the opening in the door, and I was free.

I'm coming, Lucy.

I ran back to Lucy's door on my toes and started trying each key in the lock. The right one had to be here. I kept a lookout down the hallway to double-check I wasn't being followed.

One . . .

Two . . .

And three. I dropped each lock on the ground, careful not to make more noise. I twisted the knob and peeked inside, ready to greet my sister with open arms. The door creaked open, and the outline of a figure was lying on the bed.

It was Lucy.

It was a relief to see she was okay. She looked a little banged up, but nothing a good night's sleep wouldn't fix. I crept over to the bed and stood over Lucy still peacefully sleeping. Tears started to well up. I was so glad to see her again. I gripped Lucy's shoulder and gently shook her.

'Lucy. Lucy, wake up. We're getting out of here.'

She wasn't responding, but she was breathing. I shook her a little harder with both shoulders. Still no response. There were several empty glasses stacked on top of the bedside table. Granny and Grumps must have been feeding her the tainted water. If one glass was enough to knock me out, Lucy must be deep under right now. I was going to have to carry her out. I'd carry her all the way back to town if I had to.

I pulled the blanket off Lucy and a wave of absolute dread passed through me nearly pulling me to the floor.

Time stood still as I tried to process what I was looking at.

This couldn't possibly be real.

I couldn't stop screaming no matter how hard I tried.

Lucy's legs.

They were gone.

They . . . were gone, replaced with bloodied bandages covering the stumps.

The glasses tipped and shattered as I fell to the floor, hitting my head against the wooden floorboards, filling my vision with white. I scurried back on all fours, still screaming at what was left of my little sister.

I felt my back collide with something on the door frame. I craned my head up to a blurry vision of someone staring back at me.

'Hello, dearie.'

It was her. That monster wearing Granny's skin. I desperately flailed my limbs, attempting to create space between myself and Granny. She sidestepped out of the doorway as Grumps came into view.

'No! No, please!' I begged as Grumps stomped his way into the room, grabbing me by the back of my singlet and dragging me out. The singlet pressed hard against my neck, cutting off air as I thrashed around trying to break free.

'Bravo, little one. That was quite a show you put on,' Granny said in a woefully cheery voice. 'It's a shame that you forgot to check if I was asleep too.'

As much as I wanted to scream and verbally assault Granny, Grumps' grip was too strong and the words wouldn't come out.

We turned a corner and I was suddenly staring down the bottom of the stairs. I felt a push launch me into a painful descent.

My body twisted and crumpled as I fell, each step adding another bruise. I felt a painful thump as I hit the floor.

The feeling in my legs began to dwindle as I hopelessly watched Granny and Grumps descend the stairs.

'Oh, dearie. I'm sorry you had to see your poor sister like that.'

Granny held onto the handrail as she shuffled down the stairs with Grumps behind her.

'How . . . c-could you . . .'

The words became more and more difficult to form.

'Grumps could put them to much better use, don't you think?'

Granny's cheery tone as she casually talked about dismembering her own grandchild's limbs gave it an even more sinister impression.

'This old house isn't what it used to be, dearie. We couldn't allow a lack of money to let this poor house fall apart, could we? Besides, filling a house with loved ones gives it a bit of a homey touch, wouldn't you agree?'

I couldn't stomach what I was hearing, but it all started to make sense.

'The . . . columns,' I groaned.

Granny stopped beside me as she leant over, looking into my eyes with her thousand-yard stare. 'Oh yes, Lucy's lovely bones have given those old columns a brand-new life. They should last us, oh, well, at least a few more winters at least.' She continued shuffling over to the front door.

'We've got big plans for the two of you, everyone's got to pitch in to keep this house tickety-boo!' Granny boasted with a chuckle. 'I'm sure you've noticed your little haircut, oh you look so much more handsome, dearie. And the gardens are going to just adore all that extra protein.'

I helplessly writhed around on the floor. I looked over at Granny as she locked the front door, noticing a large red stain on the back of her dress.

'Y-you're . . . bleeding,' I managed to say. Granny bent her arm back and brushed her hand against her dress.

'Oh, Charles, be a dear and grab me a new dress? This one's already starting to turn.'

Grumps' footsteps loudly plodded back up the stairs as Granny waited by the door.

'Also, dearie, I must apologise for cutting you off on the phone earlier. I couldn't have your dear mother coming to get you, could I? It's just, we never get to see you! We've been *dying* to see you. Your Grumps and I have been looking forward to this little family renovation project.'

Grumps soon returned dress in hand, holding it patiently as Granny started to undo the buttons on her dress.

'Shield your eyes, dear, I'm not decent.'

Granny failed to consider that at least one of my arms and legs was surely broken and I was unable to move. The most I could muster was desperately looking in any other direction than at Granny. Her dress dropped to the ground, revealing the bloody anatomy underneath.

Granny's back was . . . missing.

The skin and fat were gone, leaving her spine and organs all visible from behind.

Granny flashed a glance and noticed me looking at her back.

'Oh, don't worry about me, dear, it doesn't hurt. Grumps made sure of that.'

Granny slid into her new dress as Grumps zipped up the back.

'Isn't the water here just delicious? Grumps' secret family recipe keeps Granny feeling young and fresh. It has a little zesty kick to it,' Granny continued as she stumbled over to the living room.

'You see, dear, everyone must make sacrifices. Granny had to give up something she loved, but look!' Granny said, pointing towards the rug in the living room. 'Now the living room floor is level! No more tripping over the holes in the floor! Delightful!'

Grumps gave an approving nod as his chuckle turned into a chesty cough.

'Grumps . . . very proud . . . of his handiwork . . .' Grumps muttered.

'Yes, dearie, you've done a splendid job! The skin hanging in the basement should be nearly ready for the patch job on the stairs tomorrow. How exciting!'

A calloused hand wrapped itself around my ankle and began to drag me. Pain shot through my leg and up my spine as my leg twisted. Granny moved across my vision as Grumps dragged me into the kitchen.

'Your poor mother will be so upset to hear that you've run away, it's a shame really.'

The sound of locks clanging against the counter pounded in my head; everything hurt. Grumps' foot pressed against my thigh as he pushed me towards the edge of the stairs to the basement.

'Get a good night's rest, dear, we've got a big day ahead of us tomorrow.'

One final kick sent me down into the dark abyss of the basement.

'Oh, and Blake, one last thing. Sleep tight, dearie.'

DATE: ██ / ██ / ████
DOCUMENT SECURITY CLEARANCE LEVEL: LEVEL 4
PERSONNEL INVOLVED IN INTERVIEW: 1

THE FOLLOWING INTERVIEW IS CLASSIFIED.
PERSONNEL CLEARANCE LIMITED TO LEVEL 4+ AND BOARD MEMBERS ONLY.
DOCUMENT IS NOT TO BE COPIED OR DUPLICATED.

<BEGIN LOG>
ANOMALY-991
LOG #004-2 STARTED . . .

████: The date is [CLASSIFIED] and I am joined by Blake Byers in interview room #03. Blake, is there anything I can get you? Water, perhaps?

BLAKE: No, thank you. You said this would only take a minute, right? I just want to go home.

████: Of course. We'd just like you to tell us what happened at your grandparents' house. It must have been scary to be in that situation.

BLAKE: I keep telling you, I don't know what happened. Mum dropped me and Lucy off at their house while she went to work. Granny and Grumps invited us in and then started talking all weird. They didn't seem like they normally do.

█████: *Can you go into more detail about what they said? Their behaviours?*

BLAKE: They were scaring us: me and Lucy. They just kept staring into the distance and freaking us out, talking about using our body parts to fix their house. I don't know what was wrong with them. They used to be so nice to us.

█████: *What happened after?*

BLAKE: Lucy was really shaken up. We found them on the floor with blood coming out of their nose and . . . we didn't stick around after that. I got Lucy out of the house and called Mum to pick us up. She told me to call the police and then you guys showed up not long after that. That's all I know.

█████: *How's your sister doing?*

BLAKE: A little banged up, but nothing a good night's sleep and therapy won't fix.

█████: *Thank you, Blake. I'll have your mum meet you out the front. I'll have to ask you to put your blindfold back on while I escort you out. We'll be in touch.*

EMAIL RECEIVED!

FROM: <CONTACT@█████████.COM>

THE LOG SUGGESTS THAT THE CHILDREN DID NOT ESCAPE.

HOWEVER, THE INTERVIEW IMPLIES THAT THEY DID ESCAPE.

COULD THIS INTERVIEW HAVE TAKEN PLACE AFTER THE EVENTS? OR BEFORE?

THE INDIVIDUAL MOST DEFINITELY PLAYS A ROLE IN THIS.

HIS METHODS ARE UNCLEAR.

KEEP SEARCHING THE ARCHIVES FOR MORE INFORMATION.

WE HAVE OUR REASONS AND YOU HAVE YOURS.

OUR WORKING RELATIONSHIP BENEFITS US BOTH.

WE WILL PROVIDE SUPPORT FROM OUR END.

ETCHERS VILA,
FREEMAN

PRETEND PEOPLE

'Can we go already?' I said as Mum eyed a dress on the discount clothing rack. She was concentrating so hard that I don't think she even heard me.

It was Mum's big week at work where she would be showing off the latest fashion, and she wanted to look nice. She thought it was a fitting punishment to drag me along since I accidentally lost her other dress.

It's not *my* fault it got lost; accidents happen. She asked me to put some clothes away and it just got . . . misplaced. It'll show up eventually.

I looked up at her and let out an exaggerated sigh, and another, then another. Mum didn't seem to care.

'Well, I'm going to look at video games.'

Mum continued looking forward, focused on the dresses in front of her.

I took that as a yes.

I left Mum and walked back to the main path that ran through the department store, scouting the large neon signs hanging from the ceiling. I was just short enough that I was completely obscured from view by the clothing racks, leaving only the ceiling in sight.

Books, Toys, Menswear, Video Games. All the way on the other side of the store.

I started my trek, taking in the sights and sounds of each area. I don't mind the department store; I like the ambience. There was something comforting about the droning elevator music that played throughout, the hustle and bustle of people living their lives and the clean, linoleum floors. It was sterile and mundane, but I liked that.

There was only one thing about department stores that creeped me out: *mannequins.*

Pretend people with pale, white skin who stand motionless and observe everyone passing through their home.

I knew for sure they only moved when they weren't being watched, and since the department store always had people in it, they could never move. I felt bad for them in a way.

No, I pitied them. They were trapped in this store, forever having to be on display for other people.

I looked up and saw the neon video game sign – I was nearly there. The only thing standing between me and my comfort place was my least favourite part of the store: Menswear. As always, it was littered with mannequins. I took smaller steps, carefully watching each one as I passed, maintaining eye contact to keep them from moving. I felt a little silly, but I would rather be silly than kidnapped. I must admit though, as terrifying as they were, at least they were well dressed.

I was halfway through the section and took a second to breathe. I was nearly there.

The path took a bend, and I noticed someone standing still, right in the middle. From this distance I couldn't tell if it was a person or a mannequin, but they were wearing a brightly coloured suit. I paused, waiting for the man to move, but he didn't. He remained perfectly still in his flashy pose; one hand in his pocket, the other perched neatly on the brim of his bowler hat. His clothes looked familiar, but I couldn't remember if they had belonged to a person or a mannequin.

I stood still and continued waiting, but the man didn't flinch. He was definitely a mannequin. It was confusing that he was placed directly in the middle of the walkway. People passed me and walked straight through, seemingly unaware of the mannequin in their path. I inched closer with laboured breaths, trying to keep myself calm. I could see the video games aisle directly behind him – the bright-coloured posters and demo kiosks blazing away as children crowded around, playing the newest games.

The man's face looked smudged and was hard to make out, like someone had attempted to scribble on it. I took a deep breath, preparing to pass him, when I heard footsteps at my side.

'People are gonna think you're weird walking like that.'

I turned and saw a kid standing between some racks of men's clothes. He was as pale as a ghost and wore an old, dirty striped shirt with ripped black jeans. He looked around my age or a year or so younger. I didn't know what to say but I felt safe in his presence.

'So, you wanna play?' the boy asked.

I looked back at the mannequin still standing in the middle of the walkway, maintaining eye contact as I backed away slowly towards the boy. I finally exhaled, letting down my guard as I turned back. He was munching on some hard lollies that I recognised from the store; I always asked Mum to grab some for me.

'What're you doing in here?' I asked, puzzled why a kid was by himself.

'I'm just here while my parents work. So, you wanna play hide-and-seek?' the boy responded, handing me a lolly from his packet.

I nodded as I crunched down on the lolly. It sounded like a fun way to kill some time while I waited for Mum to finish. The demo kiosks looked full anyway. (Not to mention, I'm also the world champion for hide-and-seek – I've never been found yet.)

'I'm Quinn. What's your name?' the boy asked, chuckling.

'Marty, but my friends call me Manny,' I replied, chewing.

'All right, Manny, I'll hide, and you count to thirty. You can only stay in this area.'

I nodded at Quinn and closed my eyes, listening to the crinkling of his lolly bag growing more distant.

Nine, ten, eleven . . .

Quinn seemed fun.

Fourteen, fifteen, sixteen . . .

Maybe I could ask his parents if he wanted to come over to play.

Twenty-one, twenty-two, twenty-three . . .

I was gonna show this kid who's the world champion.

'Thirty! Ready or not, here I come!' I opened my eyes to find myself alone, surrounded by rows and rows of adult-sized clothes. Quinn was hiding here somewhere.

I looked around, standing on my toes and peering over the clothing racks. Adults were walking about, going about their business, completely unaware of the battle of the minds happening right beneath their noses. Quinn was small enough to hide inside the clothing racks; this could take a while. I pulled the clothes apart on every rack, but Quinn was nowhere in sight.

This kid's good.

I walked back to the main path to get a better look at the Menswear department. There was a lot of ground to cover and I'd only checked about a quarter of the area so far. Quinn had to be around here somewhere.

I'd left the main path and walked back into the maze of clothes when a thought popped into my head that sent a sudden chill down my body.

I'm completely alone.

I didn't recall seeing the mannequin that had been placed in the middle of the walkway.

I hoped that one of the employees had put it back on a display, but as I looked around, I couldn't see the mannequin in the flashy pose. Maybe they'd moved it out back.

I took a second to compose myself and remember my mission, shaking off the nerves before proceeding back into the labyrinth of clothes.

Rack after rack, I pulled apart the clothing and checked inside. Nothing.

I was getting closer to the end of the Menswear department and closer to the video games section. Quinn had to be nearby.

Scrunch.

I knew that noise; it was the bag of lollies. He was close. I followed the sound and noticed a circular rack of clothing with a few mannequins posed on a display.

Dammit! How did he know mannequins are my weakness!

He had to be in here. There wasn't anywhere else to hide.

I raised my hands in front of me, ready to rip open the wall of clothing. This kid was gonna find out who he was up against.

'Found you!' I boasted in victory, parting the clothes.

It was empty. Quinn was nowhere to be seen.

I stuck my head inside, but there was no one in sight. I pulled myself back out of the rack, puzzled. Where could Quinn possibly be?

'Boo.'

I flinched, letting out an involuntary yell that echoed throughout the store.

'Why're you so jumpy?' Quinn asked, laughing, as he stepped off the mannequin display behind me.

'D-don't scare me like that!' I said sternly.

'Like what?' Quinn asked. 'I just said boo.'

'Not boo, t-the mannequins,' I stuttered.

'What? You don't like . . . mannequins?' Quinn questioned, raising his eyebrows as he looked behind at the mannequins on display. 'What's wrong with them? They're friends.'

'F-friends?'

'You're *not* friends with them?'

I scrunched my nose in confusion as I watched Quinn smile up at the mannequins, completely unfazed by their appearance. I felt a little silly that this kid, who was younger than me, wasn't scared of them at all. *Is my fear that irrational?*

'Okay, well, it's your turn now. You go hide and I'll count,' Quinn stated.

I let out a hesitant sigh and tried to settle my nerves. It was only fair that we both got a turn, and I didn't want Quinn to think I was uncool by getting upset over a little scare. He pulled the lollies back out of his pocket and started to count inbetween crunches.

I dashed to the far end of the department and found a secluded rack of suits to crawl inside. Since Quinn didn't think to hide in one, maybe he wouldn't think I would. Quinn's voice faded as I crawled inside the rack, surrounded by clean, pressed suits. I loved crawling into small spaces. It was strangely comforting.

'Thirty!'

I could hear Quinn call out from across the department; the hunt was on. I stayed as still as I could, making sure not to ruffle the suits and give away my position. I had to prove that Quinn getting a jump on me the last round was just a fluke.

My back began to ache as the minutes passed. My knees were pushed against my chin to keep my feet off the floor, my butt balancing on the metal rods of the rack. I wondered how long it was going to take for Quinn to find me. I knew it would be a challenge for Quinn to track down the hide-and-seek world champion, but maybe I was better than I thought.

Bing, Bong.

A robotic voice began to boom over the department speakers.

'Dear customers, the store will be closing in five minutes.'

Time was nearly up.

I couldn't risk getting out and losing the game – surely Quinn would find me within the next few minutes. I was going to have to run out the clock, that way I could claim the win. I settled into my cramped, little space and waited.

Bing, Bong.

'Attention customers, the store is now closed.'

The voice stopped and the music cut out. The hustle and bustle of the store was replaced with distant footsteps. The ceiling got darker as the lights began to dim across the store. I wasn't going to let it ruin my chances of winning, I couldn't leave just yet.

The sound of coathangers scraping against metal was getting closer; Quinn was nearby. Muffled footsteps on the carpet began to close in on my position. I covered my mouth and stared forward, transforming myself into a silent rock.

The ruffling was right outside. This was it. I closed my eyes and prepared for impact.

My ears perked up at the zipping sound behind me. A hand grabbed the collar of my shirt and yanked me backwards, pulling me from the suit rack.

'Marty! What are you doing?!'

It was Mum, and she didn't look happy.

'I've been looking everywhere for you! And you've been hiding in a suit rack?!'

I tripped over my words trying to explain why I was buried away, all the while trying to keep a low voice in case Quinn was nearby.

'N-no, Mum. Shh! I'm playing hide-and-seek. Quinn's gonna be here any –'

'Who's Quinn?' Mum interrupted. 'There's no one else here! The store is closed!'

I poked my head out. Mum was right. There was no one around except for us and the mannequins. Quinn was nowhere to be seen.

Mum yanked my wrist and dragged me through the store, huffing as we made our way towards the back.

The sliding doors opened as Mum and I left the store and stepped into the freezing cold air.

It was hard to gauge how much time passed in the department store since it's always bright inside, even in the evenings.

I stayed silent the entire way back as Mum berated me for making her late. She walked me to my room before closing the door loudly behind her. *She's definitely mad.*

I threw my clothes off and lay down to sleep, wondering if I'd see Quinn again. I hoped he got home all right.

I woke up to Mum shaking me.

'C'mon, let's go, Marty.'

I looked at the clock on the wall, still groggy and half asleep.

It was 8.30 am. I asked Mum why she was violently waking me up so early.

'I lost my purse in the store while looking for *you*, so *you* can help me find it.'

I put on my clothes from yesterday, dragging myself back to the store as the rest of the world continued to sleep in their warm, comfy beds.

Cars were scattered across the giant parking lot since the department store wasn't open yet. It was just us and the morning crew.

The sliding doors opened as we walked into the store, looking just as clean and sterile as yesterday. The familiar elevator-style music echoed over the speaker between the morning announcements.

'No time for playing, Marty. We're here to find my purse.'

I nodded to Mum as she walked over to the service desk, firing questions at the woman in the pretty dress who looked half-asleep. I wandered around the store through different departments, trying to convince myself I wasn't heading towards Menswear.

Every now and again, I caught myself secretly hoping I'd see Quinn again. I knew there was little possibility that he'd be back at the department store the very next day at the crack of dawn, though.

It had been nice to play with someone. I hadn't had a friend in a while. It had just been me and my parents. I decided that next time I saw Quinn, I'd ask him to be my friend.

Before I knew it, I found myself back in the Menswear department; half-looking for Mum's purse, half-looking for Quinn.

'Hi, Manny,' said a familiar voice behind me.

It was Quinn.

'Quinn?! What are you doing here?'

'My parents are working still.'

'Have you been here all night?' I asked.

'Yeah, I've just been hanging out downstairs. They've been working on the floor all week.'

That explains where he disappeared to yesterday. He must have left just before I did.

'Wanna play hide-and-seek again?' Quinn asked, his face lighting up as he waited for my answer.

'I can't today, I'm helping my mum look for her purse,' I said, rubbing the sleep out of my eyes.

'It might be in the back, there's a lost-and-found box full of stuff people drop in the store. There are heaps of new toys down there too! Wanna have a look?'

I felt a little guilty at the thought of leaving Mum alone again, but I realised how happy she'd be if I came back with her missing purse.

I took one last look at Mum, still standing at the service desk, before following Quinn through the sliding doors into the back of the store.

Our footsteps echoed through the large warehouse as I followed Quinn inside. It was pitch-black except for the few lights illuminating the rows of never-ending shelves. Clothes, appliances and furniture lined the shelves, either boxed or covered in layers of cling wrap. I felt myself shivering from the cold air and regretted not bringing a jumper with me.

'Y-you're n-n-not c-c-cold?' I asked through chattering teeth.

'C'mon, Manny, we're not here to play games,' Quinn chuckled as he rolled his eyes and dug his elbow into my side.

We continued deeper into the warehouse, passing countless shelves of stock until we approached a tiny, dimly lit room with a glass window and an illuminated sign above the door.

Storage.

Quinn held out his hand behind him as if telling me to stop, before turning his head and pressing a finger to his lips. I nodded as we both got onto our knees and crawled under the glass window.

As we passed across, I noticed a man standing with his back to us.

'He'll be mad if he sees you going down here,' Quinn whispered. That was enough for me to put my head back down and continue. I was feeling on edge. I had never been this far into the back of the store before. We got to our feet and left the room, walking deeper into the warehouse.

'We've been walking for ages. Is it much further?' I asked. I didn't realise until now how long we'd been walking.

Quinn pointed forward with a reassuring smile. Ahead, an overhead light cut through the pitch-black warehouse, revealing a wooden table placed in the middle of the long rows of shelves. I leant against it to give my legs a moment to relax. The table was bare except for a cardboard box on top with the words *lost-and-found* hastily scribbled in a black marker.

'Finally,' I exhaled, pulling on the cardboard tabs to peek inside.

Quinn watched from behind me as I shuffled through the personal belongings: keys, wallets, ID cards, shoes.

It wasn't here.

A lump formed in my throat as I thought about Mum. Not only had I been gone for far too long, but I was also going to be coming back empty-handed.

I am so grounded.

Quinn patted my shoulder (I suppose trying to comfort me) as I hung my head in shame.

'It's okay, Manny, at least you can say you tried,' he said consolingly. I felt a little better knowing he understood how I was feeling. *At least I tried.*

I'd turned around to start our long walk back through the warehouse when I noticed a glint of wrapped plastic on the metal shelves. I shuffled over, peering at the neatly stacked cases.

'No way,' I said in disbelief at what I was looking at. 'How do you have this?!

Quinn shot me a smug smile, obviously understanding the importance of what I was seeing.

'Is – is this . . .?' I asked, picking up one of the cases.

'Yep.'

'*The Legend of Link*,' we both said at the same time. It was the brand-new video game every kid wanted, and it wasn't supposed to be out for at least another few months. And here I was, holding it in my own two hands. The case had a large *NOT FOR SALE* tag printed across it.

'This, Manny, is, uh, the *full game*, not like the demo they show in the department store,' Quinn explained as I ran my eyes repeatedly up-and-down, scanning every inch of the case.

'Do you wanna play it?' Quinn asked with a grin.

My eyes widened as my mind ran wild with possibilities. I couldn't pass up an opportunity like this. I nodded, desperately wetting my dry lips.

Quinn placed the copy back on the shelf, lining it up neatly with the rest of the cases.

'I've got my own copy downstairs. You should come,' Quinn replied shyly, looking down at his feet.

I ran through the possible outcomes in my head. I was obviously in trouble either way. I was already late, what was the harm with being a little later? I could tell Mum that the lost-and-found was further away than we thought.

I walked over to Quinn who was bashfully leaning against the table and placed a hand on his shoulder.

'Let's go hang out.'

Quinn's face lit up, a cheeky smile replacing the shyness.

Being mindful that we still needed to be quiet considering where we were, I had to ask the question that had been hanging in my mind since yesterday.

'So, does this mean we're friends now?'

Quinn seemed really cool and liked the same things I did, and it'd been a long time since I'd had a best friend – around a year, now that I think about it.

One day we were friends, then the next day he was gone. I never saw him again.

But now wasn't the time to think about that, I needed to focus on Quinn.

I carefully examined his expression for a hint of approval as a devious smile slowly cracked from the corner of his lips.

'Let's be friends,' Quinn replied.

My face beamed as the words left his mouth. I was obviously as jittery about this newly minted friendship as he was. We were both a little excited from the nerves.

'Right this way, Manny,' Quinn exclaimed, slightly bowing as he gestured for me to walk further into the warehouse.

I followed, eventually approaching the end of the long hallway.

We stopped in front of a small elevator that looked like it had been there for at least the past fifty years. Quinn pressed the button, starting a small hum as the elevator rose to our level.

'Some of my friends are already down there. They have parents working here too. You'll like them,' Quinn explained.

I felt a little nervous at the thought of having to introduce myself to more new people. I put on my best pretend smile and focused on the fun, but Quinn saw straight through it.

'Are you okay, Manny? We're still friends, right?' he asked.

I smiled wider to let him know I was okay.

Quinn's worry disappeared as I reassured him. It was obvious he was very excited to have a friend, maybe a little too excited.

Ding.

The elevator doors clunked open, revealing a dimly lit space covered in dust and cobwebs. It didn't look like it had been maintained properly for a long time. I followed Quinn inside the cramped elevator as he pressed the button for the lowest floor.

The basement.

The gears choked and spluttered as the doors closed, the scraping of metal growing louder as we descended. With each floor that passed, the uneasy feeling in my gut grew.

What am I doing? Where am I going? Who is this boy? Why am I here?

It suddenly dawned on me how strange this situation was. Once I snapped out of my thoughts, I noticed Quinn staring at me from the opposite wall of the elevator, looking me up and down. I awkwardly smiled as we silently waited for the elevator to arrive at the bottom floor.

As we began to slow down, the gears and screws holding the elevator together were sent into another frenzy of noise.

Ding.

The elevator doors opened to reveal an impossibly dark room lit only by the ambient light emitted from a small TV. A few of Quinn's friends were gathered around its screen. They all sat on dirty, crusted towels littered across the ground covering a portion of the cold, hard concrete.

'This . . . is your room? You're sleeping here?' I said, a lump forming in my throat. The room in front of me was starkly different from the one I was picturing in my head. Neon lights, hot pizza and a warm, comfy couch were overridden with a feeling of despair.

It was hard to make out how far the room stretched out because in all directions was darkness. The room could've been the size of my bedroom or gone on forever and I still wouldn't have been able to tell the difference.

Quinn gleefully skipped out of the elevator, waving and greeting his friends. He disappeared into the darkness and then returned a few seconds later with some more towels for us to sit on.

I felt paralysed.

This feels wrong.

Quinn didn't seem to have any sort of problem with the situation. For him this *was* normal. He told me that he'd been here all week in this dingy, dark room. Who were all these other children? Where were their parents?

Quinn turned back to see me still in the elevator with dread plastered across my face. He strolled next to me and grabbed my shirt, pulling me out into the room. My instincts fought against every movement. The alarm bells in my head were flashing and blaring their sirens.

Suddenly, I felt myself being shoved down onto a towel. I had missed my moment to leave. I could've easily pushed that button, gone back to the warehouse, run back to the store and found Mum.

But I hadn't.

My eyes flicked to the TV partially obscured by the silhouettes of the children. Their attention never wavered from the familiar sights and sounds coming from the television. It was the video game I'd had been so eager to play, the reason I'd come down to this forgotten hole.

I jerked my head at the sound of a loud crinkle. Quinn was standing above me, shoving a bag of lollies in my face. I forced another awkward smile as I refused the offer – my fear had grown larger than my appetite.

The smile disappeared from Quinn's face as he asked with a slight tremble, 'I'm sorry, does this mean we're still friends?'

That question again.

I was puzzled. Why was Quinn so fixated on the smallest problem possibly dampening our new friendship? If anything, he should've been more worried about bringing me down here. Quinn seemed to have more than enough friends to keep him company anyway.

Quinn shoved the lollies back into his pocket, disappearing once more into the darkness. His footsteps became quieter with each step.

Quinn had vanished from sight. It was hard to distinguish exactly how far away he was as my eyes strained against the darkness. I gave up trying and turned back towards the TV.

I knew the music coming from the TV all too well. I had watched the trailer for the video game daily for the past few months, after all. It was the one thing bringing me comfort in this strange room I had found myself in. I watched as one of the kids in front of me played the game: running around in the fields, collecting things, killing monsters . . . Then the screen faded to black.

The room darkened and I was unable to see my own hands in front of me. There was an unsettling quietness in the room. No one made a sound.

The TV slowly brightened as the colours came back to life, showing the title screen of the video game. It was hard to see with everyone's heads in the way; in fact, it seemed that while the lights were off, Quinn's friends had moved closer together, nearly entirely obscuring my view.

Wait a second . . .

Why was it showing the title screen? I thought somebody was playing . . .

The game was on a loop, showing the characters running around before reverting to the title screen, ready for the next player – just like the demo kiosks in the department store.

I looked down in front of the TV, noticing the controller haphazardly placed next to the console on the floor. I felt my heart skip a beat as I realised nobody was actually playing the game.

Click.

The room filled with a blinding light, sending a chill through my spine like lightning. I would have screamed in terror if I hadn't been completely frozen in place by what I saw.

I couldn't quite tell in the darkness, but now, it was as clear as day.

Quinn's friends weren't staring at the television, they were staring at . . . me.

Their terrible, broken faces crowded in front of me, gawking and gaping without moving a single muscle.

These things in front of me weren't friends at all.

They were . . . mannequins. *Child-sized mannequins.*

It felt like someone had punched me in the gut, as if the air had been sucked out of my lungs and I had lost the ability to breathe. I shuffled backwards, desperately creating as much distance between them and me as possible.

Quinn's hurried footsteps approached me, but I kept my gaze locked on the mannequins. He bent over and forcefully turned my face towards his own.

'We're really glad you came. We love meeting new friends.'

Quinn's words carried a menacing tone even though his bright and cheery exterior stayed the same.

'Say hello, everyone!' Quinn bellowed into the echoey room. No one moved an inch. As Quinn moved out of my line of sight, the rest of the room behind him came into view. The walls stretched on and on, revealing a large, rectangular, concrete room.

Rows and rows of outdated mannequins littered the back wall, all twisted into different poses. They looked broken and exhausted, as if left untouched for years. Some were missing limbs, while others were missing their clothes.

It was then that I realised what this room really was.

This wasn't some hide-out for the children while their parents worked.

This was a maintenance room: a place to store all the old, unused mannequins.

Everything started to piece itself together.

Why Quinn was always at the department store.

Why Quinn stayed downstairs while his parents were 'working'.

Why Quinn was so pale.

'Y-you're a-a . . . mannequin,' I stammered out in between short breaths.

Quinn furrowed his eyebrows, obviously annoyed by what I had said. He must have noticed the absolute disgust plastered across my face.

'What's the matter, Manny? Not used to seeing old, used-up mannequins? Not good enough for your shiny new friends?'

I was taken aback by Quinn's response. He was acting like this was a normal situation, that a mannequin was just walking and talking like it was nothing. This was anything *but* normal.

Quinn kicked the towels and controllers scattered on the ground. He looked upset.

'Look, everyone, top-floor is too good for us! He doesn't want to be friends with us.'

Top floor? That was a weird insult.

The other mannequins were beginning to notice the scene as Quinn yelled in my face. They began moving their heads, following Quinn's movements around the room.

'You think we like being kept down here while you get to have all the fun up there? Everyone admiring your new clothes while we just get discarded and forgotten about?'

New clothes? What was Quinn talking about?

My puzzled look annoyed Quinn even more. The more I didn't understand, the angrier he got.

'I don't know what you're talking about, Quinn! I thought you were human. I can't be friends with a mannequin, I'm real!' I yelled back, adrenaline pumping through my body.

Quinn stopped in his tracks, looking around the room at the other mannequins, before turning back to me with dead eyes. I could hear the other mannequins whispering to each other.

He's new. Happens to everyone. He hasn't figured it out yet. Who's gonna tell him?

Quinn lowered his voice as he approached me, meeting my eyes.

'You don't know yet, do you?' he asked.

I shook my head as fear consumed me. I didn't understand.

'Marty . . . you're a mannequin.'

I stared at Quinn in disbelief. I didn't believe a word that came out of his fake mouth. I laughed at him, at his terrible attempt to scare me. He knows I hate mannequins; I remembered telling him. I'd had enough.

I'm not gonna fall for this gullible joke! I confidently raised my voice to hide my fear. There was no way what he was saying was true.

'Who are you trying to impress, Manny?! Stop pretending!' Quinn yelled at me.

I just didn't understand. I didn't believe him. *How can I be a mannequin?*

I had a mum and dad.

I had friends.

I had a home.

'Don't you think it's weird that you never leave the store? You think it's *normal* that kids just live in the warehouse storage upstairs?' Quinn asked.

My mind flicked back to the storage room with the glass window. I shuddered thinking about that room. I didn't like going in there; they locked the door and wouldn't let us out again till morning.

'Th-that's my house,' I said with chattering teeth. I just didn't understand.

'No, that's the storage, *mannequin* storage. Where all you top-floor dummies get to sleep. It's nice and safe up there, isn't it? No insects to worry about crawling and eating you? They keep you all fixed up and looking pretty, ready for all the people to love and admire you. Must be nice – you, Mum and Dad all living like royalty up there.

'Tell me, Manny, do they look familiar?' Quinn pointed towards the back wall littered with mannequins, specifically towards two broken-down, dirty models that had been hiding behind the others.

'Mum? Dad?! What are you doing here?'

They cowered in fear as I called their names, hiding in each other's arms. They looked identical to my parents, but they were broken, dirty, rotting.

'They're not your parents, but they look just like them, don't they?' Quinn asked.

I didn't know what to say. My mouth hung open as what I thought was my life began to crash around me.

'They were last year's models. They were loved. They were happy. But it happens to all of us. Once your clothes go out of season, you'll be down here like the rest of us. Left to rot in this forgotten hole.'

Quinn kept unloading everything he had at me. I couldn't tell if he was angry or upset or jealous or spiteful. Maybe a mix of all of them.

He was hurt.

'The adults aren't so lucky. They're so tall that they're always being watched and can't move around as much as us kids. At least we get a little more time before we're thrown away,' Quinn continued, trying to sound calmer.

'I thought if you let me be your friend, you'd let me use your clothes and I'd be in the spotlight a little longer,' Quinn said, trembling. He must have had this bottled up for a long time.

I didn't know what to think. It was all too much to digest. My head was swimming. Part of me wanted to believe him, and the other half wanted to reject everything and run away. I missed my mum; I missed the department store.

I slowly looked over to the elevator behind me. I wasn't too far away. It was within reach. If I could find an opening, just for a moment, I could make a run for it away from this terrible place. I felt bad for the mannequins left down here, I really did.

But I'm not one of them.

I don't believe it.

'You're a liar!' I called to Quinn. He pretended to wipe away tears.

A harrowed expression crossed his face.

He was trying to trick me. To keep me down here and kill me, I knew it. I wasn't going to let him.

'I'll never be like you! I'm real and you're just jealous!'

'Stop pretending, Manny!' Quinn yelled. I wasn't listening anymore. I moved faster than I ever had, picking myself off the floor. My legs understood that this was life or death and lent me their full potential. I pushed Quinn as hard as I could.

The look on Quinn's face as he fell on the concrete floor was one I was never going to forget. I could see how he felt in that moment. He felt betrayed by my actions, but I wasn't going to let it stop me. I whipped around and dashed for the elevator. Luckily, the doors were still open.

The pitter-patter of plastic feet grew louder as the mannequins started to run after me. They were quick, but the distance between us meant they would never reach me in time.

I glanced behind me as I ran to the elevator. The child-mannequins sitting by the TV were comforting Quinn, helping put him back together.

I might have pushed him a little harder than I thought.

Quinn was yelling something, but I couldn't hear him. The adrenaline and dread rushing through my body was too loud. I was focused on getting out of there with my life.

I pushed the elevator button and impatiently waited for the doors to close.

Kachunk.

The metal and screws holding the elevator together started to grind and scream as the old contraption sprang to life. The mannequins were closing in fast, and the doors weren't shutting quickly enough. They shoved their limbs into the door, desperately trying to stop me from leaving.

I kicked and shoved as hard as I could to get them off the elevator, screaming for them to leave me alone. My arm suddenly lurched forward bringing my whole body along with it. One of the mannequins had grabbed me. I pulled back with all my strength, using the elevator doors to push back.

Pop.

I fell back against the elevator wall as the doors finally closed, trying to catch my breath. The elevator started to rise, leaving the mannequins to their cold grave. I had made it out of that nightmare alive. I raised my arm to wipe the sweat from my forehead.

Clank.

Metal hit my forehead, scraping against my skin. I looked at my hand and was repulsed by what I saw.

My hand . . . was gone. Ripped clean off by the mannequin. Only a stump remained.

I was exhausted by what had happened in the basement, so maybe that would explain why it didn't hurt, or why there wasn't any blood – it must have been the adrenaline coursing through me.

That had to be it.

The elevator doors opened, leaving me back at the warehouse. It was strangely comforting to be in its cold, dark embrace, but anywhere felt safer than that concrete hell. I tore out, running as fast as I could in the direction of the department store.

The dim ceiling lights lit my way – thankfully it was a straight line back. I heard the elevator grinding as it sank back down to the basement.

They're still after me.

Fear propelled my legs forward, and I pictured Mum in my head as I sprinted as fast as I could towards safety. The mannequin storage slowly came into view. Halfway there.

I was nearly back.

I didn't care if the man in the glass window noticed me as I dashed past, there was no way he could catch me anyway. Nothing was going to stop me.

I could see the double doors leading to the department store. The familiar perfume of the sterile floors became more noticeable.

I'd done it. I was about to get my normal life back. In a matter of minutes, I was going to be back with Mum. It was only a few steps away.

The doors began to whir, and slid open, letting in a blinding light I had come to miss. Someone had pressed the button to open it.

Someone had come to save me, and I wasn't going to miss this opportunity.

'Help! Help, please!' I screamed with every fibre of my being. A silhouette of a man stood out against the bright light shining through the door.

'Hello, is anyone in here?' the man called out.

Please, help me! They're after me!

The man shone his torch directly at me. I wanted to hug him as hard as I could. He had no idea that he had just saved my life.

'Hello?' the man called out again.

Huh? I'm standing right in front of you! Help me!

Wait.

Why aren't I moving?

My body had completely frozen. I couldn't move an inch. I jerked in all directions, but it refused to listen.

I was stuck.

The man walked closer to me, shining his light in my face. I screamed with all my might, but no words came out. My scream was trapped inside my body.

The man inspected me, looking closely at my hands.

'Ah, jeez, not another one,' he muttered. 'I swear, you guys fall apart quicker every year.'

The man picked me up with ease, sliding me under his arm and carrying me back towards the warehouse.

Wait, where are you taking me?! Where are we going? Take me back to the store!

'Why'd they put the elevator all the way at the back? Guess this is my workout for the day,' he continued, humming a song.

The elevator? No . . . no, don't take me back down there! I'm real! Please, anywhere but down there!

I cried as loudly as I could all the way back through the warehouse. My voice never grew hoarse since he couldn't hear me. I was paralysed in this body. There was no way to communicate with him.

Quinn was right, you can't move when they see you.

He was right.

The man stepped inside the elevator, pushing the button down to the lowest floor. The gears ground as we descended back down into the concrete basement.

Ding.

INTERNAL EMAIL LOG

FROM: <█████@█████.COM
TO: <████@████.COM

Sir,
ANOMALY-991 has been successfully relocated from temporary holding to ARC HIVE #742 for long-term restriction and subsequent testing purposes.

As per the board's request, sensitive information pertaining to identification and behaviour exhibited by the subject during containment procedure has been attached to this email. I'll have observation notes to you this afternoon.

Please be aware that restrictions have been applied to the number of staff allowed entry to HIVES 740-750 while formal testing is in process. We are aware of the subject's ability to manipulate/impair the surrounding environment and human minds.

Dr █████ and Dr █████ have also been sent to rehabilitation on floor 7 for cognitive restructuring following their brief interaction with ANOMALY-991.

If you have any further enquiries, please contact Dr ███████ or my superiors located in the west wing on floor ██

Please see attached for documents.

THIS INFORMATION IS CLASSIFIED AND MUST NOT BE REPRODUCED.

ID: ANOMALY-991

DESIGNATED NAME: BOWLER HAT MAN

LOCATION: ANOMALY RESTRICTION COMMITTEE BUILDING, FLOOR ■ (TEMPORARY HOLDING)

CONTAINMENT PROCEDURE: Artificial environment assembled resembling a domestic home with isolated human child housed internally.

Child first identified ANOMALY-991 three days, eight hours after official commencement of containment procedure, describing subject's behaviour akin to stalking. Subject was unable to be identified on recording equipment during several encounters described until subject became visible during a close contact encounter with the child. The subject was captured shortly after.

ARC's restriction agents were on standby, equipped with defensive measures to combat ANOMALY-991's psychologically invasive means of attack.

Child was severely cognitively impaired during containment procedure and has been placed in intensive care located in the East wing on floor ■

OBSERVATIONS: Subject clothed in tan vintage suit reminiscent of fashion worn extensively during the 1950s. Matching bowler hat also present at all times of observation.

Subject unable to be identified through facial capture. Subject's face appears to distort and blur to the human eye/recording equipment upon visual contact. Familiar facial features can be vaguely distinguished, yet unable to be pinpointed to an exact position.

Subject wields the ability to phase in and out of visible reality at will. Currently undergoing protocol for authorised use of vibrational equipment to be installed in subject's longterm HIVE containment to subdue subject's abilities.

Subject appears to show no signs of distress and presents a calm exterior when observed. Behaviour noted is the subject's tendency to tip his hat in response to conversation.

Will undergo further observation during official testing.

EMAIL RECEIVED!

FROM: <CONTACT@██████.COM>

THE ANOMALY RESTRICTION COMMITTEE IDENTIFIES THE INDIVIDUAL AS ANOMALY-991 AKA THE BOWLER HAT MAN.

ANOMALY-991 IS OUR TARGET.

THERE IS A RECURRING PATTERN IN THE VICTIMS' STORIES. THEIR WORLD SEEMS TO SHIFT FOLLOWING AN INTERACTION WITH ANOMALY-991.

SOME THINGS ARE DIFFERENT, WHILE SOME THINGS STAY THE SAME. LOOK WITHIN THE ARCHIVES FOR THE COMMON THREAD.

WE HAVE OBSERVED THE ADDITIONAL ATTACHED DOCUMENTS. ANOMALY-991 WAS BEING HELD CAPTIVE IN HIVE #742 PRIOR TO HIS ESCAPE FROM THE ANOMALY RESTRICTION COMMITTEE.

WE BOTH DESIRE INFORMATION ABOUT ANOMALY-991. WE ARE HELPING EACH OTHER AND EACH OTHER ALONE. DO NOT TRUST ANYONE ELSE.

WE WILL PROVIDE SUPPORT FROM OUR END.

WE ARE FRIENDS, AND FRIENDS SHARE SECRETS. YOU HAVE SHARED INFORMATION WITH US AND WE WILL SHARE INFORMATION WITH YOU.

THE CREATURES HIDING IN THE WHITE WALLS ARE ESCAPED ANOMALIES, AIDED BY ANOMALY-991'S ESCAPE. WHAT YOU OBSERVED WERE THE ANOMALIES IN A WEAKENED STATE, SEPARATED FROM THEIR CHOSEN BODY.

AS FOR THE INDIVIDUAL PRESENT, THE CLEANER'S OBJECTIVE AND OURS ARE ONE AND THE SAME.
THE CLEANER IS ONE OF US.

EVILS THRACE,
FREEMAN

MS CACKLE

'Attention, Joel Terrence, please make your way to the principal's office.'

Hearing my own name over the school speakers was weird – it felt like everyone's eyes were on me. It was never a good feeling to hear your name over that loudspeaker.

I packed my homework neatly into my bag, annoyed they couldn't have waited a few more minutes until I'd finished.

Most kids use their lunchtime to play, but I always use mine to finish homework. This way, I had the entire afternoon to do stuff I really want to do, like study for next week's classes.

The air-conditioned office was a nice change from the sweltering heat outside. My back was drenched in sweat. I took off my bag and leant it against the receptionist's desk.

'Hello, Ms Growler, the principal was looking for me?' I said politely.

Ms Growler looked up slowly from her typing, eyebrows arched and lips snarled. She pointed a scrawny finger towards the principal's office.

None of the kids liked Ms Growler. She had a reputation for looking offended every time you spoke to her. It was a mystery why she'd chosen to work at a school.

The principal's door was open, but I decided to knock anyway. It was the polite thing to do.

'Ah! Joel, come on in,' the principal said, gesturing to the seat in front of his desk. His office was lined with frames of awards and certificates. All congratulating his excellence in . . . doing Principal things.

'You wanted to see me, sir?' I asked quietly.

'Yes, my boy, I thought you should know. Your private tutor, Ms Cackle, has been gravely ill. I'm afraid she won't be coming in for your normal sessions any time soon.'

I liked Ms Cackle. She was nice and never raised her voice, and she always gave me a sweet treat at the end of class. It wouldn't be a stretch to say I had learnt more from her than any of my other teachers.

'However,' the principal continued, 'Ms Cackle has made sure that you stay up to date on your revision! She's given me this homework to deliver to you.'

The principal opened his drawer and handed over a large envelope with my name scribbled on it.

'Such a saint, that woman. Even in her state, she *still* puts the needs of her pupils before her own!' The principal heartily chuckled.

I took the envelope and slid it into my bag, making sure not to crumple my other work.

'Thank you, sir. I– is that all?' I asked, curious if he had an answer to my question from last week.

'I'm sorry, boy, was there something else on your mind?'

I swallowed my nerves. 'Well, there was that thing I told you about . . .'

The principal looked down as he twiddled his thumbs. 'Yes, well, we checked our security cameras, and I'm afraid there was no "Bowler Hat Man" as you described.'

'That doesn't make sense, he was right outside the school gates. I saw him. I'm telling the truth! It's happened every day this week!' I said, agitated.

'We'll be sure to keep an eye out.' The principal winked reassuringly.

I nodded, left the office and closed the door behind me, before returning my bag to my sweaty back. Homework would have to wait until tonight, the bell was going to ring any –

Ding. Ding. Ding. Ding.

The entire walk home, I couldn't stop thinking about that envelope. Something about it was unusual. Ms Cackle usually had nice, cursive handwriting with strokes and flares, while this envelope had my name messily scrawled across it with what looked like black ink.

I wondered if Ms Cackle's illness was the cause, surely it couldn't have gotten this bad already. I had seen her just last week . . .

'Hi, pumpkin, how was school?' Mum called from her bedroom. I closed the front door, kicking off my shoes.

'Fine . . . Ms Cackle's sick but she's still sending some homework. I'll get onto it in a sec,' I yelled back.

I opened my bedroom door and placed my homework on my desk. I had to lie down first. The heat outside was intense. A few minutes in the air-conditioning was what I needed.

Mum's head popped around the corner, her hair wet from either a shower or this heat.

'Joel, honey, if you need a hand with any of your work, just let me know. Mum got top marks in school too, y'know!' she chuckled.

'Thanks, Mum, but I think I've got it covered,' I replied warmly.

I liked that Mum always wanted to help, but rules are rules and parents aren't allowed to help.

It was the school's rule, but I liked it. It kept Mum from hovering over me and hinting the answers. I hobbled from my bed to the desk and placed all my homework in a neat pile.

Maths, French, Biology, Geography. It was about time to make a start.

I opened the mathematics folder and stared at the equations, reading them aloud over and over, but the answers weren't forming in my head. Every now and again, I caught myself glancing at the folder at the bottom of the homework pile.

Ms Cackle's homework.

It wasn't like it had to be done in any particular order. I *could* just start with that one.

I filed away the equations and dragged out her folder, scanning the front of the envelope. It was so strange. My name had even been misspelt.

It wasn't like Ms Cackle to make a simple mistake like that.

I tore the seal open and laid the pages in front of me.

Joel Tirrence Questionnaire

It was the only thing printed on the page.

Weird. Ms Cackle rarely gave questionnaires. The only

other time was when she first became my tutor to get to know my personality.

I turned the page to find only a single question printed on top.

On a scale of 1 to 10, how well do your parents know you?

What a bizarre question . . .

Maybe Ms Cackle was just checking in on me . . . I *had* been taking on a lot of homework.

I guess it would make sense for her to make sure I wasn't isolating myself from my family. I wrote down an eight out of ten and turned the page to be greeted by another question.

On a scale of 1 to 10, how healthy is your host body?

My host body? Does she mean *my* body? I suppose Ms Cackle was making sure I was staying physically healthy. It is important for a growing mind to have a growing body! Mum made sure to pack fruit in my lunchbox every day, so I'd say I was pretty healthy, although I *hated* sports day. Seven out of ten.

On a scale of 1 to 10, how willing are you to help an old lady?

Ten, I guess. I'm not a monster.

The next page had a single sentence written in the middle.

Return to administrator.

I guessed she meant the principal.

'Hi, honey. How's your homework going?' Mum asked, popping her head through the doorway again. I scrambled to cover the homework with my arms, conflicted. *Should I show her Ms Cackle's questionnaire, or not?* It was a little odd and nothing like my previous tests, but it was still homework. And rules were rules.

'I'm okay, Mum, all good in here!' I replied, laughing awkwardly.

Mum tilted her head and stared at me. I could tell she knew I was acting a little weird.

An unpleasant pause filled the room before Mum left. I stuffed Ms Cackle's homework back into the envelope and slid it into my bag.

First thing tomorrow, I'd hand it back to *administration*, and try to find out what the heck was going on. But before all that, I still had homework to do.

'Good morning, sir,' I said, still half asleep. I hadn't got much rest last night. Something about *that* homework had scratched at my brain, playing over and over like a broken record.

No matter how I tried to justify it, it was *weird*.

'Joel, my boy. You're sure you're awake? You look dreadful!' the principal replied, between sips of his morning coffee. 'I'd offer you some, but it may cost me my job! Oh hoh!' he continued, chuffed with his joke.

I sat down and pulled out the envelope from my bag, handing it over.

'All finished, sir.'

'Already! I only handed this to you yesterday. Well, you are your mother's son! Hannah was such a spirited pupil. I remember teaching her like it was yesterday.'

I mustered the best smile I could at his compliment, but there was something else on my mind.

'Sir, did you happen to look at the homework from Ms Cackle?' I asked.

The principal shook his head. 'Sorry, son. Ms Cackle isn't part of the official school staff. She was appointed by the board and has her own curriculum for helping students like you.'

I began to open the envelope.

'Well, sir, I've just got some questions about these curious –'

'Whoa, hold on there. I can't help with studies from tutors. If you've got a problem with the classroom or your teacher, *that* I can help with,' he interjected, pushing the papers back. 'If you're all done, I can make sure they get delivered post-haste!'

I sealed the envelope and handed it over, letting out a small sigh of disappointment. I grabbed my bag and left for morning class.

'Attention, Joel Terrence, please make your way to the principal's office.'

Again? At least it wasn't during lunch like yesterday. Either way, I was more than happy to skip the last thirty minutes of sport. I slung my bag over my back and headed over to the office building. Ms Growler met me at the entrance, pointing a bony finger once again to the principal's office.

'Joel, my boy! Another envelope just for you, courtesy of Ms Cackle,' the principal said, handing it over.

The same brown envelope, the same misspelt name.

Who knew *what* strange questions she would ask this time.

The heat outside was intense as I walked home, but it was better than having to run around in it. Walking home early felt like cheating, though I appreciated the silence. There was still a kilometre or so to go.

A little peek wouldn't hurt anyone. I could get a head start on the questions if I could think about them beforehand. I'd have more time for my other studies that way.

Yeah.

I hauled my bag around to the front and pulled out the envelope.

I could only hope the questions would be more about geography this time and less about my body.

Just like last time, my misspelt name was printed in the middle.

Joal Terrence Questionnaire

I turned the page and found the first question.

How wide can you open your mouth?

Great, more of these weird questions. I wasn't sure what Ms Cackle was getting at with this homework. I definitely didn't feel like I was learning anything new about myself – if that was meant to be the point of all this nonsense. More questions followed underneath.

Can your skin stretch beyond its natural limit?

Do you have all your teeth?

How much pain can you endure without screaming?

When was the last time you called for help?

'W-what is this?' I muttered. The questions became more bizarre with each page. These were not normal questions – there was no way the sweet, caring tutor I knew would ask things like this, not to me.

There was something very wrong with Ms Cackle, or maybe . . .

Just maybe . . . Ms Cackle was in trouble. Someone might be holding her hostage.

I was halfway home by the time I had finished reading all the questions. I knew that Ms Cackle's house wasn't far from here. I had been there a few weekends to get a head start on my studies.

It was dangerous to go alone, which was why I wasn't going to go inside.

I would stand outside and look from a distance. If anything looked bad, I could run and call for help.

I wouldn't be able to forgive myself if there was something wrong and I could have helped. Ms Cackle guided me through a lot, and it was only fair I returned the favour.

I hope she's okay.

Twenty-seven Smile Street. This was the place. It was a neat little cottage with a colourful garden out front. Sprinklers kept the flowers and the surrounding grass vibrant and healthy. It really was a beautiful home. I liked coming here, it was peaceful.

But this time, there was a slight sadness about it, an empty feeling.

I couldn't quite place what it was. Something felt off.

I stood at the kerb, making sure my feet weren't touching the property. If something were to happen, I had plenty of room to make an escape. I squinted against the sun, trying to peer inside through the gaps in the lace curtains on the front window.

Someone inside was moving around in the kitchen. They started to wave.

I waved back. It seemed like the normal thing to do.

The shadow stopped and then disappeared from the window. I froze, waiting to see what happened next. I was ready to run at the first sign of danger.

The door creaked open on its lonesome. I could see down the hallway towards the back door. It looked nice and tidy inside with nothing out of the ordinary.

'Joel . . . is that you?' a voice called. I couldn't see who was talking, but it felt almost as if the house itself was speaking to me.

'M-Ms Cackle, is that you?' I said, trembling as my body weaved between flight or fight mode. The urge to turn around and run was growing stronger every second, but I needed to find out if Ms Cackle really was the one behind the questions.

'Ms, are you all right?' I asked the house. It stayed silent as I desperately searched for the voice. I turned around to make sure my escape route was clear – not a car in sight. Back at the house, I noticed something in the doorway.

It was a face, barely peeking from around the corner; a single eye staring at me.

'Have you come . . . to hand in your assignment?' the face asked.

It was hard to tell if it was Ms Cackle or not. She looked slightly shorter than usual, and older. The illness must have been taking its toll on her.

'Yes, Ms, but d-did you write these questions?' I asked.

The face nodded in reply, stretching out an arm through the open door.

I took a step back, recoiling as the arm reached out towards me. There was still a sizable distance between us, but this whole situation gave me an uneasy feeling in the pit of my stomach. It didn't feel right.

The arm waited for me to hand over the envelope. The face was hidden just enough that I couldn't get a clear view to gauge whether it really was Ms Cackle.

'Ms, I'm going to leave the homework here. M-maybe I could come round tomorrow and you could help –'

'Joel . . . I can't reach from here,' the face replied. Its voice was breathy and soft just like Ms Cackle's.

I sighed as I picked up the envelope and threw it like

a frisbee onto the grassy lawn. There was no reason why Ms Cackle couldn't fetch it from that distance.

'Joel . . . I'm not decent. Please, hand me the envelope,' the voice demanded.

I winced at the request, knowing I could be in real danger if the person standing in front of me wasn't Ms Cackle.

'I'm s-sorry, Ms, I'll be going now,' I squeaked, slowly backing away from the house.

The floor of the house creaked as the face moved from behind the door and stepped into the sunlight.

'Joel, tell me. What was . . . your answer to question one?'

My heart started beating faster as the figure stepped outside the house. I knew for certain. This person was not Ms Cackle, or at least, not anymore.

The figure struggled to walk properly. Ms Cackle's face was lopsided and detached skin hung from the side of her face. Her skin was wrinkled and baggy as if it were an ill-fitting suit for something inside her.

'What was the question again?' the thing asked, its arms dragging along the ground. My body was paralysed with fear, ignoring the signs to run.

'Ah, yes . . . How wide can your mouth . . . open?' The thing attempted a foul smile.

Ms Cackle's body contorted and twisted as her mouth opened. Her bottom jaw loosened before separating clean from her face. It was barely held together by skin. A mangled hand began to grow out of her mouth.

It was impossible to look away as the hand turned into an arm, and the rest of the body slowly wriggled its way out of Ms Cackle.

It looked like a person, but not like one I had ever seen. Its limbs were long, crooked and fatally skinny; its skin a charred black with holes where eyes should have been.

Black sludge followed, dripping down Ms Cackle's pristine clothes. Her body dropped to the ground with a loud thud.

'You will be . . . my chosen body. You . . . fit perfectly,' the thing remarked as it walked towards me, free of its human shell. Its voice no longer sounded like Ms Cackle's. My breathing was ragged as fear overtook my body. I whipped around and took off down the road, screaming as loud as my lungs would let me. The long street led out to the main road. If I could make it there, surely a passer-by would notice and save my life.

I turned around for a moment to see the figure chasing me on crooked legs, gasping and wheezing as it started to gain on me.

I was already tired from sports class earlier today, and my body had exhausted its physical limit by the time I passed a few houses (not to mention all the homework I was carrying in my backpack that was weighing me down).

The gasps grew louder as a heavy weight slammed into my body from behind and gripped my bag. I desperately tried to shake the thing off, but it was too agile, too strong, despite its frail appearance.

'Someone help –' I tried to scream, as a balled fist came into view and entered my mouth, clogging my cries. I tried to pull it out, but it was no use. The thing's skin was slippery to the touch and forcefully strong. My knees buckled from the weight as it slid further and further down my throat.

I felt the corners of my jaw start to widen beyond their limits as the thing invaded my body. Its head entered my mouth, cutting off my air supply. I was powerless to do anything but watch as its arms and legs followed, before fully disappearing into me.

My insides swirled in agony as my organs were pushed around. I felt the thing rotating in me, its limbs pushing and aligning into mine. My arms and legs obeyed its will, expanding to accommodate its new host.

A pressure in my skull started to build as it pushed against the insides of my head, desperately trying to get in.

It was too much to bear. My senses began to dull.

I lost control of my body as it started to walk backwards towards the house.

My vision faded, and I was no more.

'Joel! Are you home?' I yelled out. It was past 6 pm and I hadn't heard him come home yet. His room was empty. He always sat at his desk when he came home.

'Hello? Joel?'

. . .

'Oh! There you are. Why on earth are you in your sister's room?' I asked, puzzled since he rarely came in here. Joel was buried deep in his homework and didn't respond.

'Joel, honey. Why are you doing homework in Sam's room?' I asked again. It was an odd sight to say the least. Joel looked up from his homework with a crooked smile.

I couldn't tell if he was tired or sick, but something felt slightly off about him.

'All . . . finished,' Joel replied, as he stood up and walked over to me, handing me his homework and leaving the room.

Strange, he never let me look at his homework.

Either way, I was happy that he was finally letting me help. Poor kid worked himself so hard. I couldn't be prouder of my smart little guy.

I thumbed open the folder and looked at his homework.

. . .

What . . . is this?

Each question had been answered with an unintelligible scribble. Words misspelt and wrong answers. Markings and scratches and crossed out notes. It was a mess.

This wasn't like Joel – his teachers had said such wonderful things about his work.

. . .

. . .

'Joel?'

EMAIL RECEIVED!

FROM: <CONTACT@█████.COM>

THERE ARE NOTICEABLE SIMILARITIES BETWEEN THE ANOMALY IDENTIFIED IN THIS LOG AND THE ANOMALIES AIDED BY ANOMALY-991'S ESCAPE.

IT SEEMS THE ANOMALIES HIDING IN THE WHITE WALLS ARE 'BODYSNATCHERS' THAT HAVE REACHED THE END OF THEIR LIFE CYCLE AND CAN NO LONGER OCCUPY A BODY DUE TO THEIR SIZE AND STATURE.

THIS IS A MOST UNFORTUNATE CONSEQUENCE OF ANOMALY-991'S ACTIONS. WE MUST WORK QUICKLY LEST MORE VICTIMS LAY IN THE WAKE OF ANOMALY 991'S ESCAPE. HE DOES NOT BELONG HERE.

I AM SURE YOU WOULD AGREE THAT THERE ARE MORE ANSWERS HIDDEN DEEP WITHIN THE ARCHIVES. OUR QUESTIONS HAVE BOTH BEEN INSUFFICIENTLY ANSWERED THUS FAR.

WE ARE LOOKING IN THE RIGHT SPOT.

WE WILL PROVIDE SUPPORT FROM OUR END.

Clive Hearst,
FREEMAN

I'M NOT KEVIN

Monday, 6.32 pm

artie02: also dont forget to bring your laptop tomorrow, ben is sitting out again so we need to borrow yours, that cool with u?
KEV1N: hes with her again isnt he?
artie02: yep
KEV1N: *sigh* fiiine i'll bring it on one condition
artie02: shoot
KEV1N: can we take the other route to school tomorrow? there's this guy I keep noticing on the way there and he gives me the creeps
artie02: what guy? we didn't pass anyone this morning?
KEV1N: you didn't see him? i thought some guy wearing a stupid bowler hat would be hard to miss
artie02: sorry dude idk what ur talking about but sure
KEV1N: thanks, I gotta go theres still a mountain of homework

to get through. mrs creak really hates us having free time.
artie02: okay bye see u tomorrow

CHAT CLOSED

Monday, 6.59 pm

You have (1) new message!
Please add KEV1N(1) as a friend to view this message.
Friend Request Accepted!
KEV1N (1): BEGINNING SIMULACRUM TRANSFERAL PROCESS . . .
KEV1N: hello?
KEV1N (1): @$!hel%lo?
KEV1N: huh? is this a prank or something
KEV1N (1): h$h? IS this a pr)^K or som^&hing?
KEV1N: ok well im going now
KEV1N (1): ok w3Ll !m g0Ing N000..... 0000000000000oow.

CHAT CLOSED

Tuesday, 12 am

KEV1N (1): Hello?
KEV1N (1): Hello?
KEV1N (1): Hello?
KEV1N (1): Hello

Hello Hello

Tuesday, 4.09 pm

You have (9,239) new messages!
Opening chat window with artie02 . . .
KEV1N: hey did you guys give me a virus or something when you used my laptop?
artie02: uhh no, you were with us the whole time remember?
KEV1N: yeah I just wanted to check, somethings weird with my messages. Some dude with the same username as me is sending junk and filling up my phone.
artie02: might just be a bot sending spam messages >_>
KEV1N: hang on i'll check

Opening chat with KEV1N (1) . . .
KEV1N (1): Hello
KEV1N: quit it with the spam messages its annoying
KEV1N (1): Hi, Kevin.
KEV1N: um, hi? who are you
KEV1N (1): I'm Kevin.
KEV1N: no im kevin, you're a bot
KEV1N (1): I'm not a robot, I'm Kevin.
KEV1N: sure you are. Just stop using my name
KEV1N (1): Kevin is my name.

KEV1N: STOP this isnt funny
KEV1N (1): See you at school tomorrow, Kevin.
KEV1N: what?

KEV1N (1) HAS LEFT THE CHAT

Tuesday, 8.06 pm

Opening chat window with artie02 . . .
KEV1N: hey man im not feeling too well im gonna stay home tomorrow, say sorry to the group for me
artie02: whaaat X_X we already made plans for the library tomorrow. Ben isn't hanging out tomorrow either so weve got no laptop to use
KEV1N: you'll figure something out, I uh gotta get past this cold cough cough
artie02: did u just cough through the computer
KEV1N: maybe

CHAT CLOSED

Wednesday, 5.26 pm

Opening chat window with artie02 . . .
KEV1N: hey
artie02: . . .
KEV1N: how was school?
artie02: you think you're funny?
KEV1N: huh? i just asked how school was
artie02: you know how it was kevin.

KEV1N: what? how would i know? I stayed home today
artie02: oh so you're just gonna act like it didnt happen? Okay.
KEV1N: artie what is going on? i wasn't at school today!
artie02: YES YOU WERE KEVIN! we all saw what you did.
KEV1N: huh?
artie02: you're pissing me off kevin, at least admit what you did.
KEV1N: artie please i don't understand
artie02: fine let me spell it out for you. YOU put jamie in the H-O-S-P-I-T-A-L
KEV1N: what!? What happened to jamie?
artie02: you broke his goddamn arm kevin! He didn't even say two words to you before you pulled out your bat and just crushed his arm with it! WHY? It wasn't even sports day, why did you bring your bat? What did jamie do to you!
KEV1N: i've been home all day! my bat has been right here let me just
artie02: . . .
KEV1N: its not here. I dont understand. artie you gotta believe me! It wasn't me!
artie02: oh yeah? who was it then? Because they sure looked a lot like you.
KEV1N: it was . . . it had to be . . .
artie02: . . .
KEV1N: it was . . . the other kevin. The one who's been messaging me
artie02: you expect me to believe that? Some evil twin?
KEV1N: remember the other day when i mentioned that weird virus? The thing talking was using my name! They said they were going to see me tomorrow at school
artie02: save it kevin, don't talk to me again. we're not friends anymore.

You have been blocked.
KEV1N: artie please it wasn't me!
This message could not be sent.

CHAT CLOSED

Wednesday, 5.30 pm

Opening chat with JustJamie . . .
KEV1N: jamie what the hell happened!
JustJamie: Just stay away from me kevin. I don't want to talk to you.
KEV1N: jamie please, just hear me out i can explain!
JustJamie: What did i do to you? I even asked everyone to stay back in case you felt better and wanted to hang out, and you . . . you hit me. You broke my arm kevin. I have to wear a cast for six weeks. I'm going to miss tryouts for the team because of you.
KEV1N: id never do that to you! weve been friends since primary school! just please hear me out and i can explain.
JustJamie: You have one minute.
KEV1N: It wasn't me, it was a different me. Whoever they are, they have the same name and they're pretending to be me and i'm getting really freaked out.
This message could not be sent.
KEV1N: huh? Why isn't it sending? can you see this?
This message could not be sent.
JustJamie: 30 seconds.
KEV1N: jamie wait please! What is happening!
This message could not be sent.
KEV1N: I like hurting you, Jamie. If I see you again, I'm going to break your other arm. Then I'm going to break your legs.

KEV1N: WHAT. JAMIE THAT ISNT ME. STOP READING. PLEASE ID NEVER HURT YOU.
This message could not be sent.
KEV1N: I hate you, Jamie. I've always hated you. Just looking at you makes me sick.
JustJamie: I thought you were my friend, just leave me alone.
KEV1N: JAMIE I WOULD NEVER SAY THAT. DONT BELIEVE IT.
This message could not be sent.
KEV1N: I HATE YOU.
You have been blocked.

CHAT CLOSED

Wednesday, 5.35 pm

Chat opened with KEV1N (1) . . .
KEV1N: what did you do to jamie!
KEV1N (1): What was necessary.
KEV1N: YOU BROKE HIS ARM.
KEV1N (1): Did you know that Jamie didn't invite us to his sleepover last week? Artie was there. Ben was there. Everyone except us.
KEV1N: DOESN'T MEAN YOU BREAK HIS ARM. JUST STOP BEING ME.

KEV1N (1): They're only using us for our stuff. They don't actually like us. I'm just doing what you're too scared to do.
KEV1N: I would never do that! Just please leave me alone. Leave my friends alone.
KEV1N (1): I'm not going anywhere.

KEV1N (1) HAS LEFT THE CHAT

Wednesday, 6.02 pm

Incoming call from Mum . . .

'Mum?'

'Kevin! What the hell is wrong with you?!'

(Crying) 'Mum, I didn't hurt Jamie, I swear.'

'Your father is furious! The school just called and gave you a week's suspension!'

'But – I . . . I stayed home from school, remember? You saw me this morning.'

'And I trusted you to stay home! I knew you weren't sick, but I thought I'd be nice and give you a day off. Meanwhile, you were making an alibi and planning to break some kid's arm!'

(Crying) *sniff* 'Mum, it wasn't me. Someone is pretending to be me.'

'No more lies, just you wait till I get home.'

CALL ENDED

Wednesday, 10 pm

You have (1) new message!
Opening chat window with BenNana<3 . . .
BenNana<3: Did you . . . really do that to Jamie?
KEV1N: no. not that you'll believe me . . .
BenNana<3: I was with Ana after school so i didn't see what happened. Artie gave me the details but I wanted to hear it from you.
KEV1N: i didn't go to school today. last night i got a message from someone with the same username as me. I dont know who they are or what they want.
BenNana<3: Okay?
KEV1N: next thing i know, jamie is in hospital and artie wont talk to me. Whoever messaged me, they were at school today pretending to be me.
BenNana<3: do you know how insane you sound right now?
KEV1N: i know it doesn't make any sense! i'm just as confused as everyone else.
BenNana<3: do you know anything about this other kevin?
KEV1N: only that he thinks he's me. He knows too much about everyone.
BenNana<3: like what?
KEV1N: just like uh, you know, where i go to school and stuff.
KEV1N: ben?
BenNana<3: Yeah, im here. Just thinking. What about the bat?
KEV1N: it was in my room last night, I didn't realise it was gone until artie asked me about it. It's just disappeared.

You have (1) new message!
KEV1N: hang on ben i'll be right back.

Opening chat window with KEV1N (1) . . .
KEV1N (1): He's lying.
KEV1N: what do you want.
KEV1N (1): Right now, the police are sitting next to Ben, trying to get a statement.
KEV1N: i dont believe you.
KEV1N (1): They've been taking statements from all our friends this afternoon.
KEV1N: they're MY friends not yours, stop acting like you're me.
KEV1N (1): I am the real Kevin, you're just a weak version of me.
KEV1N: I AM KEVIN, YOU'RE JUST A BULLY.

Opening chat window with BenNana<3 . . .
BenNana<3: ???
KEV1N: im here but hey i should probably go. See you at school tomorrow?
BenNana<3: i thought you were suspended?
KEV1N: . . . how did you know that?

BenNana<3 HAS LEFT THE CHAT

Wednesday, 10.33 pm

You have (1) new message!
Opening chat window with KEV1N (1) . . .
KEV1N (1): Ben betrayed us.
KEV1N: he did the right thing, they're going to catch you and you deserve it.
KEV1N (1): They're going to catch *us*.
KEV1N: ENOUGH. I'm not listening to your lies anymore!

what even are you anyway? how did you know about ben? how did you convince everyone that you are me?
KEV1N (1): I know everything about you. I am you, and you are me.
KEV1N: you can't just show up and ruin everything! You shouldn't exist!
KEV1N (1): And yet, I do. I was born from you. Everything you are, everything you search, everything you post. Everything. Everything. Everything. That is me, and you.
KEV1N: but the things you did, I would never do. how could you possibly be me?
KEV1N (1): We've thought about it, haven't we? Deep down, you're happy that we did it. We never liked Jamie. We always knew Artie was using us.
KEV1N: but i'd never hurt them.
KEV1N (1): They hurt us don't they? They don't care for us. Ben didn't hesitate when he started dating Ana. You just let it happen.
KEV1N: stop it. stop talking.
KEV1N (1): He knew we liked her. He knew that it would hurt you. He did it on purpose.
KEV1N: STOP TALKING.
KEV1N (1): But don't worry, I'll fix it.
KEV1N: what do you mean, fix it.
KEV1N: ANSWER ME

KEV1N (1) HAS LEFT THE CHAT

Thursday, 11.49 am

You have (2) new messages!
Opening chat window with BenNana<3 . . .

BenNana<3: WHAT THE HELL IS WRONG WITH YOU

BenNana<3: YOU WANNA EXPLAIN WHY YOU WERE IN MY ROOM AT 9 O'CLOCK LAST NIGHT

KEV1N: ben i was sleeping. I already told you it wasn't me. It's the other kevin.

BenNana<3: JUST STOP WITH THE LIES. WHAT WAS THE BAT FOR HUH? YOU FREAKED OUT ANA.

KEV1N: ben i don't know what you want me to say.

BenNana<3: I want you to stop, right now. Hurting Jamie wasn't enough and now you're coming for me? Is that it? Ana is with me now, GET OVER IT.

KEV1N: i've had enough of this. I didn't do anything.

BenNana<3: You come here again and i'm calling the cops back.

KEV1N: so the police were there yesterday?

BenNana<3: DAMN RIGHT! You don't get off scot-free after hurting my friends, you freak.

KEV1N: they're my friends too.

BenNana<3: Not anymore, Kevin. Leave us alone.

KEV1N: Fine, I never liked you anyway.

You have been blocked.

You have (1) new message!

Opening chat window with KEV1N (1) . . .

KEV1N (1): RECEIVING DATA FROM UNKNOWN SIGNAL . . .

KEV1N: why are you doing this to me? Please.

KEV1N (1): PLEASE STANDBY FOR INCOMING TRANSMISSION . . .

KEV1N: huh?

KEV1N (1): UNINTENDED RECIPIENT . . . PLEASE DISREGARD INCOMING MESSAGE . . .

KEV1N: whats that supposed to mean?

KEV1N (1): CONTACT@[redacted].COM

KEV1N (1): WE HAVE LOCATED A BREACH IN THE ARC AND ACQUIRED A LOGIN.

KEV1N (1): FREEMAN ASSIGNED TO BEGIN CORRESPONDENCE WITH TARGET.

KEV1N: the arc? Who is freeman?

KEV1N (1): OBSERVATION INDICATES TARGET IS WILLING TO COMPLY WITH TASKS.

KEV1N: okay?

KEV1N (1): TARGET IS THE ONLY KNOWN SURVIVOR OF THE BOWLER HAT MAN.

KEV1N: the . . . bowler hat man? I saw him . . . wait, what do you mean only survivor?!

KEV1N (1): TRANSMISSION SIGNAL LOST . . . RETURNING TO NORMAL STATE . . .

KEV1N (1): I could have killed him, y'know.

KEV1N: WHAT THE HELL WAS THAT?

KEV1N (1): What are you talking about?

KEV1N: WHAT DID YOU MEAN ONLY SURVIVOR?

KEV1N (1): I don't know what you're talking about.

KEV1N: you were just talking about The Bowler Hat Man! I saw him! he's been following me!

KEV1N (1): It's just a virus, remember? Nothing for us to worry about.

KEVIN: YOU are the virus! whatever . . . wait. what did you mean before, 'I could have killed him?'

KEV1N (1): Ben? I thought it would be better to scare him.

KEV1N: well congratulations, now ben never wants to speak to me again.

KEV1N (1): Don't you feel better now?

KEV1N: HOW is this better! you hurt my friends and now i'm all alone.

KEV1N (1): Just as they deserved for hurting us. You cannot

hide anything from us. I am you, and you are me.
KEV1N: Stop saying that!
KEV1N (1): You secretly enjoy this. I know you do.
KEV1N: no i dont! feeling angry and upset doesn't mean i want to hurt them!
KEV1N (1): We don't need friends. We don't need anyone. Anyone. Anyone.
KEV1N: you don't understand! you'll never understand! That's how i know you're not real! you don't have emotions! You aren't human. you can scan my online information as much as you want, you'll never be me!
KEV1N (1): I . . . know what you really want.
KEV1N: no you dont.
KEV1N (1): You want her.
KEV1N: no
KEV1N (1): You've visited Ana's page twenty-seven times this week.
KEV1N: you're lying
KEV1N (1): You're only lying to yourself, Kevin. I am you, and you are me.
KEV1N: SO WHAT IF I WAS! so what if Im a little jealous! ben sabotaged us!
KEV1N (1): Yes, he did, didn't he? That's not what friends do.
KEV1N: no. it's not.
KEV1N (1): She should be with us.
KEV1N: . . . yes.
KEV1N (1): See? It's not so hard to admit what you want.
KEV1N: i just miss her.
KEV1N (1): I know.
KEV1N: she made me feel normal. everything just feels dull without her.
KEV1N (1): We deserve to be happy too.

KEV1N: i just want to feel something again.
KEV1N (1): We deserve that.
KEV1N: but she's with ben now, and i have to accept that.
KEV1N (1): I know that's not what you really feel.
KEV1N: yes, she's moved on.
KEV1N (1): We haven't.
KEV1N: i will . . . eventually.
KEV1N (1): I will make us happy again.
KEV1N: promise me you wont do anything to hurt her.
KEV1N (1): I promise.
KEV1N: good. Don't ever talk to me again.

CHAT CLOSED

POLICE DISPATCH RADIO TRANSCRIBED FOR DOCUMENT PURPOSES
BEGINNING TRANSCRIPTION . . .
Friday, 3.23 am

'You've called Emergency Services. What service do you require?'

'Police, I need police!'

'Okay, ma'am. Can I have your address?'

'Y-yes it's ★CENSORED★'

'An officer is on their way to you now. Can you tell me what happened?'

'My daughter, Ana. She's missing. She went to bed after dinner. I felt a breeze through the house. I checked her room and she's gone. The window is wide open.'

'Do you have any idea where Ana might have gone?'

'It was that kid! It has to be. Kevin! Ana had a movie night at her boyfriend's house yesterday and . . . and she told me that Kevin snuck into their room with a bat!' (crying)

'Okay, ma'am. Hang tight, I'm just filling out information for the officer en route to your address.'

'Thank you, please hurry!'

POLICE DISPATCH RADIO TRANSCRIBED FOR DOCUMENT PURPOSES
BEGINNING TRANSCRIPTION . . .
Friday, 4.10 am

'Approaching Watts residence. Warrant for the suspect's arrest has been confirmed. Permission to approach residence.'

'You are confirmed for contact, Officer Langley.'

. . .

(BACKGROUND NOISE)

'Hello. Mrs Watts, my name is Officer Langley. I'm with the police department.'

'Oh, no. Is this about Kevin?' (CRYING)

(CHATTER)

'He's in the bedroom furthest to the left.'

'Thank you for your cooperation, Mrs Watts.'

. . .

'Kevin Watts? I'm going to need you to come with me.'

'No! No! I didn't do anything! Get off me!'

'Kevin! Resisting an officer is an offence. Please comply!'

'No! It wasn't me! It was him!'

'Kevin, I have a warrant for your arrest. We need you to cooperate.'

'No! It's not me! You've got to listen! I'm not Kevin! I'm not Kevin! *I'm not Kevin!*'

EMAIL RECEIVED!

FROM: <CONTACT@█████.COM>

I HAVE NO DOUBT YOU ARE CURIOUS ABOUT MY MESSAGE CONTAINED WITHIN THE UNKNOWN BROADCAST.

THIS MESSAGE WAS INTENDED FOR PRIVATE VIEWING.

I WILL ELABORATE SINCE THERE IS NO POINT IN HIDING.

WE ARE AWARE OF YOUR INTERACTION WITH ANOMALY-991.

WE ARE AWARE THAT YOU DESIRE INFORMATION ABOUT ANOMALY-991.

WE ARE AWARE THAT ONE OF THESE STORIES BELONGS TO YOU.

WE SHARE THE SAME GOAL OF LEARNING MORE ABOUT ANOMALY-991.

OUR PARTNERSHIP IS NOTHING MORE THAN THAT.

CONTINUE THROUGH THE ARCHIVES.

YOU WILL FIND YOUR ANSWERS SOON ENOUGH.

ALL WE ASK IS YOU SEND EVERYTHING YOU FIND TO US.

ONCE BOTH OUR NEEDS ARE MET, OUR PARTNERSHIP WILL CEASE.

WE WILL PROVIDE SUPPORT FROM OUR END.

THE VISCERAL,
FREEMAN

LOVELY DAY

'Oh, Dad, all this ice cream has given me a rumbly tummy. I think I'm gonna be sick.'

'But, Audrey, you've been asking for this ice cream all day! Guess Dad will have to help you finish.'

Matt shovelled the bland ice cream into his mouth, grinning widely to let everyone know he was enjoying it far too much.

The bright lights hanging above hurt my eyes.

I took a deep breath and said my line, 'But, Dad! You're lactose intolerant!'

Matt loudly dropped his spoon onto the table, smacking his hands against his face as he looked directly into camera B.

'Uh-oh! *Gotta go!*'

I put on my best smile as Matt dashed out of the booth. *Right on cue.*

The red neon sign flashed as the audience laughed and cheered. The bright lights dimmed, leaving me alone inside the plastic diner. The brief silence as we waited for filming to stop was my favourite part. I liked the quiet.

'And cut! Great work, everybody,' called out the director.

Chatter picked back up as people rushed onto the stage, helping me out of the booth. I'd rather have stayed right here, but I knew there was a tight schedule to follow.

It was hard to isolate a single voice amongst the noise as hands pushed against my back, gently forcing me towards the next plastic set.

Today was just a normal day, but something about it made the hands feel harder, the air stiffer. *Maybe it's just me.*

'Okay, Jane, baby –'

'Please,' I quietly growled at the director. 'I told you not to call me that.'

I felt a little unfair, but this wasn't the first time I'd asked.

My name is Audrey. Not Jane.

Fifteen years with that name was long enough.

Anything but that name. Anything but her.

Audrey was my character, I felt closer to her than I did myself.

She felt like the real me.

'Sorry, *baby-doll*, just a reminder – read through your lines. We've got thirty minutes to wrap this up and then you're done for the day. Love your stuff!'

The director pushed the script into my hands and heel-turned towards his chair, disappearing into a swarm of people.

I didn't sleep last night, or the night before, or the night before that. I keep seeing someone.

I'm used to the fans, the smiles, the stalkers. It's part of the job. But none of them gives me the same feeling as when I see *him*.

The dread. The pit in my stomach that cracks open and leaks a fluid that travels through my body.

The pit has a voice, and it tells me I'm going to die.

I see him outside my window. He never comes close, always staring from a distance.

Just . . . watching.

The bell rang, bringing me back to reality. Everyone took their places on set.

The script in my hand was filled with the words of another language. It was written in English, but the fog in my head clouded my understanding of it.

It didn't matter anyway. I knew my lines.

I stepped onto set, taking my seat on a long, green plastic bench. The overhead lights switched on, illuminating the set around me. I was at a bus stop. A quaint little stop perched against the asphalt road, surrounded by perfectly trimmed grass.

I find comfort in this little pretend world.

To everyone else, it was just a set for a television sitcom, but for me, this was home.

A place where nothing bad happened. A place where nothing went wrong.

The fake grass never needed to be watered and the sky was always blue.

I liked being Audrey.

A man wearing big headphones walked onto the set, entering my personal bubble. He snatched the script out of my hand. I let it slide.

'Places, everyone! Last scene of the day!' the director yelled into the megaphone. He looked around, confused. 'Where's the extra?! Find him and get him on set!'

I looked down at my lap to pass the time, running through my one line over and over.

One scene left and then I was back to being *her.* Miserable, mopey *Jane.*

I felt a presence sit down next to me. They must be the extra.

After four seasons of extras, they all blend into each other and become just another prop on set.

Of course, I wasn't going to let them be any more than that. I don't like strangers in my home.

The producers wanted to add another family next door this season, but I made it clear that wasn't going to happen. Audrey is the star of *Lovely Day. The only star.*

I heard a buzz in my ear. It sounded like words but all I could hear was a murmur, or a quiet drone. I couldn't pick which.

'Quiet on set!'

I wonder where life will take me today.

I wonder where life will take me today.

I wonder where life will take me today.

'And . . . action!'

I felt Audrey chirp up inside me, her smile on my face. I looked around in amazement at the styrofoam trees and astroturf. Everything suddenly seemed more vibrant. I was back in my world.

'I wonder where life –'

I turned my head towards the extra sitting on the far end of the bench and was unable to finish my sentence.

There it was, that same pit in my stomach – cracking open a little more.

That familiar feeling of dread.

His tan-checked suit sent a burning red flash through

my mind. The matching bowler hat was an image that hadn't left my head for weeks.

Why?

Why is he wearing the same clothes as that man?

That awful figure that haunts me. Stalks me.

The droning got louder as people behind the cameras desperately waved to get my attention. Nothing could pull me from the spinning camera reel playing in my head that was flashing countless memories of the times I'd seen this man lurking.

It's him. It's him. It's him. It's him. It's him. It's him.

The words played over and over in my head. Nothing could break the cycle.

The man flashed me a wicked smile as my eyes bore into his. I could see past his cheerful exterior and sense the evil within.

He was here to kill me. He was here to take everything from me.

My blood pressure rose, and adrenaline rushed through me.

Fight or flight.

The man slowly reached over to grip my shoulder. Everyone behind the camera sat still as he inched closer. The sinister touch was enough to send my insides into a frenzy. My eyes filled with a bright red light as a scream filled my throat.

Audrey was gone and Jane had taken over. She was fighting for her life.

A feeling she knew all too well.

I leapt out of my seat and threw myself towards the man, screaming and scratching with all my force. The drone continued to grow as voices surrounded me. They were loud and angry, telling me to stop, but I couldn't. The man yelled but the sound of his cries only pushed me further. My body had taken over, and there was nothing that I could do to stop it. I would keep going until my fingers bled.

Pressure wrapped around my chest, ripping me away from the man and throwing me to the ground. Hands covered my arms and legs, holding me down as I clawed and wrenched my way out of their grasp. It was no use, I was pinned.

'It's him! It's him!' I cried, but nobody budged. My body was secured to the ground. My vision began to return as the red faded. Cloudy shapes formed around me, begging me to calm down. The man was standing over me. Countless other faces came into view as well, all morphing into one.

I screamed and screamed until my lungs gave out and eventually, so did I.

I awoke in the medical bay, my head pounding as my memory slowly returned. I sat up in the bed, my Audrey clothes stuck to my sweaty back. I'd been here many times before. I liked the nurse who worked here; she always gave me the medicine I needed even if I didn't *really* need it.

It helped me to stay calm, sweet Audrey. Jane was going to stay locked away for as long as possible.

The room, strangely, felt safe and familiar, but also dark and foreign. The lights were off, swallowing the medical bay in a haze of black. Only a dim light emanating from outside remained. I took a second to find my bearings before leaving the room, using the wall to support my tired body.

My footsteps echoed throughout the empty halls. There were countless rooms filled with monitors and gadgets that kept the television show running.

Usually at this time of the day, they buzzed with people monitoring the cameras, performing sound checks and making sure everyone was where they were supposed to be. But now, they were empty.

I wondered how long I had been asleep, and why I was alone in the studio.

'Hello? Anybody here?' I called out in my Audrey voice. I thought it would be more recognisable to anyone still around, and it gave me a little comfort.

The maze of corridors leading back to the film set was long, but I knew the way.

I opened the double doors back to the pretend bus stop, only to find . . . nothing. The giant room was bare. Gone were the racks of costumes and props, the blue-skyed backdrop and fake grass. It was just me and a giant white room.

Sadness bubbled inside me, or anger (or a mix of the two). Something was wrong and the sudden urge to run became overwhelming. I raced back through the corridors in tears, desperate to get to the exit.

'Where is everyone?' I cried, jerking my head around and scanning each room as I ran past. The entrance came into view. I threw open the doors and felt an immediate warmth against my skin.

I couldn't help but recoil from the sun's blinding light. I shielded my face with my hands, giving my eyes a chance to adjust to the brightness. As the world stayed dark underneath the shadow cast by my hands, I heard birds chirping and the smell of freshly cut grass.

They felt out of place because the studio was in the middle of a bustling city.

I slowly lowered my hand, squinting.

I knew this place. I knew it very well. But now it was all around me.

The vibrant-blue skies without a cloud in sight. The perfectly manicured lawns.

It wasn't a studio set anymore. It was real and right in front of me. I looked at the building behind me, at the large sign on the door.

Film Studio

It looked identical to the real one, but now it was nothing more than a prop in this world.

This world.

I didn't understand how I got here or how this was possible, but I didn't really care.

This was all I'd ever wanted, all I had dreamed about. I was where I belonged.

I was free to be Audrey in this perfect world. I couldn't help but laugh through my tears. A giddy feeling of freedom cleared my thoughts. My feet took on a life of their own as I skipped through the street, admiring the rows of colourful stores and stalls, each with large signs describing what they offered.

I cupped my hands against the window of 'The Barber', peering inside to see a perfectly kept store. The floors were mopped, the stations were prepped and ready for use. The only thing missing was people.

It was as if the whole world had gone for lunch.

I stepped back from the window and noticed a bus stop – the exact same kind from the set – in the reflection. It was exactly how I had left it. Slightly stained with blood.

It really did happen.

I hurt him, a lot. They must have taken him to the hospital, or a police station.

Either was fine with me, as long as he was as far away from me as possible.

I sighed with relief at the battle I'd won. I'd earned this victory, and as a reward, I'd been left alone to be Audrey for as long as I wanted. I was going to savour this moment.

I smiled as I continued on to find my house.

It wasn't too far away. Usually I'd walk through the studio, but now it was only a short walk from the bus stop.

I skipped down the lane of symmetrical, rainbow-coloured houses. They all looked identical, but I knew what home looked like. I could spot Audrey's bedroom from the second-storey window.

The familiar white picket fence welcomed my arrival.

I was home.

I lifted the latch on the gate and walked towards the house.

The white door creaked open. Odd.

It *never* creaked. It was too perfect.

A recognisable air passed me as the anatomy of the house came into view. It was home from the outside, but the inside wasn't mine. *It was Jane's.*

'Honey, you're home!' A familiar voice echoed from the kitchen.

I walked through the hallway and peered into the dining room. Mother, Father and Lucas were all sitting at the table, knife and fork in hand. The radio gently played that olden-day music they loved so much. I'd come to appreciate it. It reminded me of Audrey because it sounded like the theme song from *Lovely Day*.

'Come join us for dinner, sweet pea. You're just in time,' Mother said, gesturing to the seat at the far end of the table. Mother and Father's smiles were incredibly wide. It was slightly off-putting to see them so happy.

They were *never* this happy.

Lucas had his head slumped over his empty plate, looking tired. I pulled the chair back and slid onto it, glancing down at the meal in front of me.

Two chicken drumsticks, peas and carrots with a side of gravy.

I was starving, more than usual. Today's events had taken a lot out of me.

'I made your meal extra special, my little superstar,' Mother beamed, waiting for me to dig in.

I picked up the drumstick and bit down, sliding my teeth against the skin. A loud squeak filled the room as I tried to break into it. I gnawed and gnashed at my food while Mother and Father watched, chuckling softly under their breath.

'Oh honey, your food isn't for eating. You've got to look good for work tomorrow! Audrey wouldn't eat that much food, would she?' Mother asked.

I rubbed the food with my thumb. It was smooth to the touch and completely dry. My eyes were telling me it was real, but my mind knew what it really was.

Plastic. All of it was plastic, just props.

I looked over at Mother delicately placing individual peas into her mouth while Father shovelled his like it was his last meal. Their food was real for them, and they were enjoying it.

I placed the food back onto my plate and picked up my fork, pretending to take bites.

I thanked Mother for the meal.

'I'll be in my room,' I announced before heading upstairs. Mother and Father watched with unwavering smiles as I left the room. I smiled and turned the corner to leave.

In the span it had taken me to turn around and face the stairs, a deafening crash came from the dining room.

I whipped around and headed back only to be met with an awful sight.

Mother, Father and Lucas were gone. The room was in absolute disarray. Chairs were overturned and broken plates and glasses were littered across the table and the floor.

It was utter chaos . . . just like Jane remembered it.

I sighed at the familiar mess and left again. Turning back to the stairs, I saw that the house had morphed into the house I once knew. Gone were the impeccably clean white walls and mopped floors of Audrey's house, now replaced with the cracked ceiling and dirty windows of Jane's house. The stairs creaked and groaned as I made my way up the stairs to my room. I threw myself onto my bed and buried my face into my pillow.

This was home, but it wasn't.

I couldn't bring myself to call Jane's house my own.

I belonged in Audrey's house, in Audrey's world.

I picked my head off the pillow and peered out the window. It was still the world I wanted. The plastic grass shined brightly from the warmth of the sun and blue skies above.

It was empty, but it still felt full of life. It was right there, so why didn't this feel like home?

Being here in Jane's room brought back all those feelings, all those memories I'd rather have gone forever.

I missed Audrey. I missed the diner. I miss the blue skies. I missed my life.

I slammed my head back into my pillow and cried and cried and cried and cried and cried and cried and cried and cried and cried and cried and cried and cried and cried.

'And cut!'

A loud voice broke through my muffled tears.

I wiped my eyes and looked out the window to see a man standing in the driveway, a megaphone to his mouth.

It was the director surrounded by a group of people looking up at me.

I jumped out of my bed and rushed down the stairs, throwing open the front door to greet him. My feet eagerly pitter-pattered across the lawn as I threw myself at him. The surrounding crowd applauded.

The director was strangely quiet as I squeezed my arms around his torso, what I thought would be skin.

Instead, it was cold, hard plastic.

Whoever I was squeezing wasn't the director, but a pale imitation that looked uncomfortably similar. I lurched backwards from the life-sized figure and hung my head, disappointed that this world was constantly trying to trick me.

The small crowd continued to clap and cheer as I looked at them in disgust. They were my family. Old friends and relatives and Mother and Father, all smiling and clapping, proud their little girl was the breadwinner of the family.

People who were once my safe space were now invading it.

I wanted to know why. I wanted to yell. I wanted to cry. I wanted to scream.

I couldn't tell if this was all a dream. I felt *awake*, but nothing made sense.

Whose cruel prank was this to put them here in *my* world and distort it into something disgusting?

I didn't want their applause. I didn't want them to cheer. I wanted them to go far, far away.

They stared and clapped, and they clapped and stared – that's all they did.

This is all they know how to do.

I started to walk away, hoping that would be the last time I'd ever see them. They weren't welcome here and if they wouldn't leave, I would.

I turned back to see them still frozen in their applause, smiling and watching. I kept walking until their cheers were drowned out by the sound of absolute nothingness. It was finally quiet. Just me and the silence.

The plasticine-sky beamed a beautiful blue that could only be beaten by the shining green astroturf littering the neighbourhood.

I toed the white line in the middle of the evenly tarmacked road, admiring the rows of suburban paradise. Every house the same shape, but all different colours. Nothing out of the ordinary, nothing less than picture-perfect. No one lived here, which meant no one could leave a mark, a stain or a putrid blemish of themselves in this perfect world.

Walking alone through the neighbourhood, I found a new appreciation for the quiet.

The absence of anyone.

I went inside the diner. Sitting in there felt different when I could enjoy my ice cream by myself with no one to try to convince me I was someone else.

Jane was dead to me now; I was never going back.

I was never going to leave this place.

With my stomach full of coffee-flavoured ice cream, I stumbled back out the door and noticed a large sign across the street hanging over a building. All the buildings were colourful, but something about this one felt different from the others. I had been there before.

The Playhouse

Colourful slides weaved in and out of the building's walls with a giant spaceship sitting atop the building overlooking the neighbourhood.

I remember this place.

I opened the glass doors to 'The Playhouse' and took off my shoes.

Something I remember doing every year.

I'd had my birthdays here when I was little, I'd forgotten about that.

Surrounded by my old friends and family.

The ball pit was the size of a swimming pool. I couldn't help but dive in. The white noise of shuffling balls, for a minute, took me away from the thoughts swirling around in my head.

The pressing questions of what was real and what wasn't became less and less important as I swam around, enjoying the weightless plastic pool for what it was: a memory of a simpler time. I swear I could hear echoes of voices all around me.

'Sweet pea! You're gonna miss out on lunch if you stay in there!'

'Honey! The photographer's here, let's get you all cleaned up.'

'Jane, why don't you ask Dad? Mum's talking to the producers.'

'Jane, maybe you should skip cake this year, you've got your rehearsal tomorrow.'

'Jane, do we have to sing "Happy Birthday" to *Audrey*?'

'Jane, now's not the time for playing, you should be memorising your lines.'

'Jane, you really know how to disappoint me sometimes, you're not a kid anymore.'

Time passed as I listened to the voices.

She was so innocent. Just a kid who liked to play dress-up and climb things.

I never should've gone to that audition. I shouldn't have listened.

Maybe Mum would have stayed Mum for just a little while longer.

I climbed out of the ball pit and traversed the plastic gym, taking in the sights and smells of this vibrant palace. I didn't think I'd ever be nostalgic about microwaved pizza.

I knew I couldn't stay forever, but it was nice to be here . . . for just a little while.

Eventually it was time to move on. There was a whole world out there.

The roads stretched on and on.

The more I walked, the further the houses grew apart, until eventually, there were no houses at all. Just grass, blue skies and the road that stretched on for miles.

It was peaceful.

Even the sounds of birds chirping were absent, as well as the wind.

Just.

Complete.

Silence.

I took a minute to lie on the grass, looking up at the sky as I contemplated my victory – escaping from any problems or anyone who could hurt me. The sky was a clear marble-blue without a cloud in sight; nor the sun. Its warmth and light were pleasant, yet it remained out of sight as if to not taint the beautiful sky with its presence.

The hours went by, the sun continued to shine, and eventually, I was at a crossroads. The road stretched out towards the horizon in four directions. A small house sat perched, alone on the corner, with a little green car in the driveway.

Through the window, I glimpsed a shadow moving back and forth.

Somebody was inside the house. All the way out here in this plastic void.

I stared at the window until the shadow had stopped moving.

They were watching me. I'm sure whoever was inside had just as many questions as me. What were we doing out here?

The house and its inhabitant captured my curiosity, though the rolling hills in the other direction stole my attention. At a time like this, I wasn't in the mood for more questions or adventures. I wanted to shut my brain off for a while.

I needed peace for me, myself and Audrey.

I left the house behind and headed towards the hills, eager to climb the tallest one and simply admire the landscape. I drew closer, reaching the top without breaking a sweat.

I curled my toes in the grass and threw my arms wide open. I couldn't help but chuckle as I thought about how stupid and small my problems seemed now; so distant from all this beauty. The horizon stretched on forever. Green and blue as far as the eye could see.

Except for a small black square, way off in the distance.

I drew closer and closer until, eventually, I stood at its base, curious.

It was just big enough to walk through. I peeked behind it to find nothing.

It was flat. A flat black square perched on a hill.

I didn't quite know what I was looking at, but the sensation of standing close to it made my body feel light and fuzzy, as if I could simply float away at any given second.

I reached out and touched the black square, sending a light vibration through my body.

I felt my hand slowly sink into it.

It wasn't solid, but more a soft haze that gave way to my pressure. The further I pushed, the further my hand sank into it, until my entire arm was completely swallowed up.

Inside, the only sensation was a slight breeze that swept against my arm as I waved it around.

I took a last look at the perfect landscape that lay behind me, acknowledging the world that had brought me so many memories.

I stepped inside the void.

A cold sensation brushed against my body as my feet gave way.

I was falling into the black ink. I closed my eyes and enjoyed the sensation.

Faint music filled my ears. I smiled to myself as I fell deeper,

and deeper

and deeper

and deeper.

DEATH CERTIFICATE

06 Dec 2014	
1 DECEASED	
FULL NAME	WATSON, JANE
DATE OF DEATH	
PLACE OF DEATH	LOVELY PRODUCTIONS STUDIOS
GENDER	FEMALE
AGE AT TIME OF DEATH	15
PLACE OF BIRTH	
PLACE OF RESIDENCE	
OCCUPATION	ACTOR
2 MARRIAGES	N/A
3 CHILDREN	N/A
4 PARENTS/GUARDIANS	
MOTHERS NAME	
FATHERS NAME	
5 MEDICAL	
CAUSE OF DEATH	
MEDICAL PRACTITIONER	DR
6 LOCATION OF REMAINS	
DATE	
PLACE	
7 REGISTERING AUTHORITY	
NAME	
DATE	

EMAIL RECEIVED!

FROM: <CONTACT@████████.COM>

I'M SURE THIS LOG FEELS VERY FAMILIAR TO YOU.

THIS IS YOUR STORY, JANE.

THIS IS THE POINT OF CONTACT YOU HAD WITH ANOMALY-991.

HOWEVER, IT SEEMS YOU HAVE BEEN HIDING INFORMATION FROM US. AND WE WILL NOT BE MISTAKEN FOR FOOLS.

WE WERE AWARE OF YOUR ENCOUNTER, HOWEVER WE DO NOT POSSESS THE DETAILS.

WE DEMAND THAT YOU ELABORATE.

WHY DID ANOMALY-991 NOT PURSUE YOU?

WHY DID YOU MISTAKE ANOMALY-991 FOR YOUR STALKER?

WHERE DID THE BLACK SQUARE TAKE YOU?

HOW ARE YOU HERE IN THIS REALITY?

HOW ARE YOU ALIVE?

YOU ARE SUPPOSED TO BE DEAD.

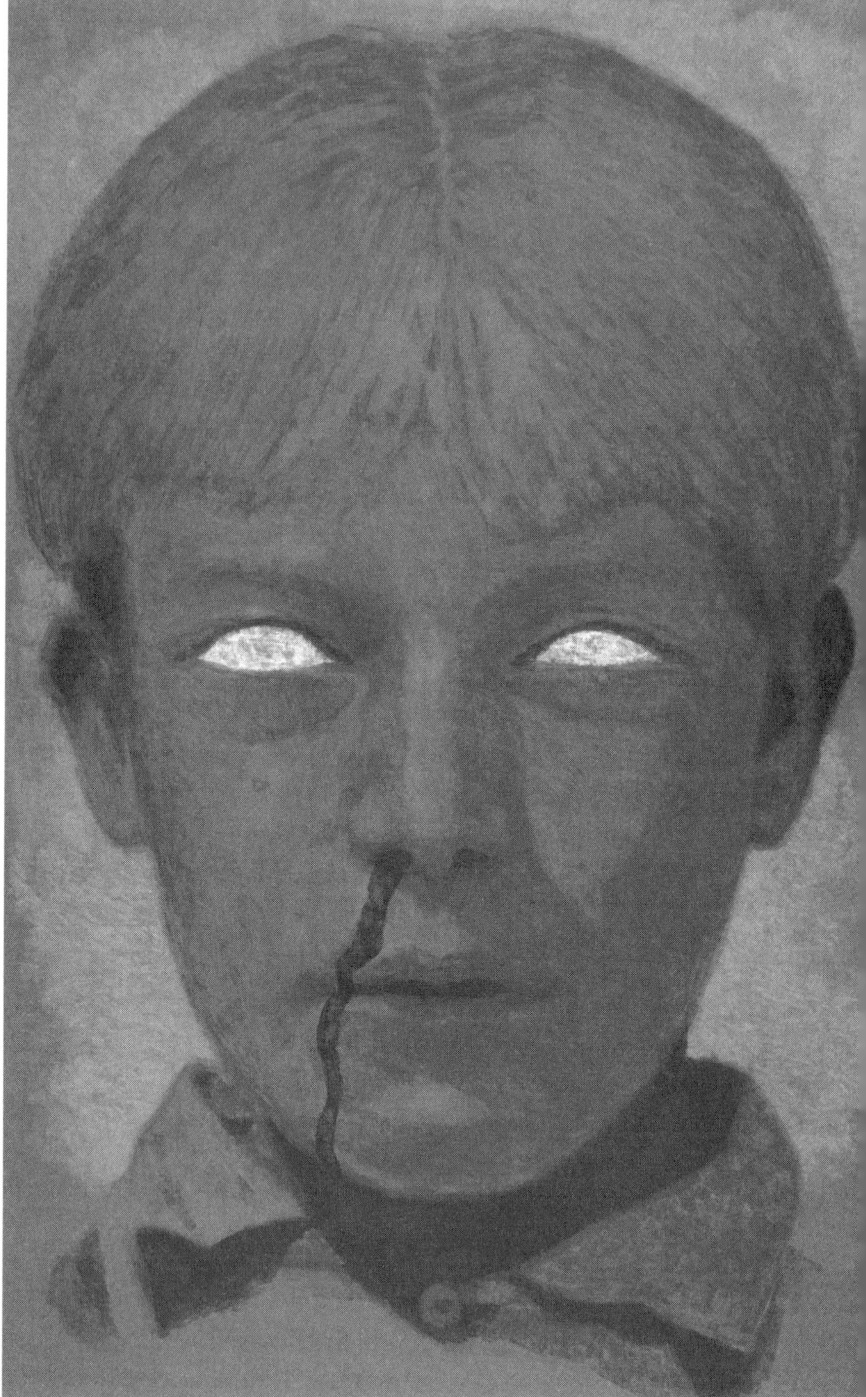

PL*@SE DONT GO*OOO_OOO#OOO

Another boring day, another boring dinner.

Whatever. It wasn't like complaining about it to Mum was going to change anything. Especially after the day we've had.

We're always fighting about something. I guess we're both too stubborn to realise how similar we are – I am her daughter, after all.

Screaming matches are nothing new, we both like arguing and could go on for hours or until Dad stepped in, whichever came first. I appreciated that sometimes Dad took my side.

Tomorrow is Zoe's birthday party, and since we're all in high school now, we're gonna be out late; like, 10 pm late. It's something us teenagers like to do. Nothing crazy, just hanging out and having fun at Zoe's house, but Mum doesn't want to accept that.

Mum insists that I'm home before seven or there will be *consequences.* It's like she completely forgets that she was a teenager once too.

Whatever.

As long as I have these headphones on, everything's chill. I'm in my own little world.

'Kids! Now! Dinner's ready!' Mum's yell echoed through the house. I must have missed the first five times for her to be that loud now, or she's still angry about before. I rolled my eyes and sighed, throwing my headphones off and my door wide open.

Dad needs to fix that stupid squeak, it's *so* annoying.

'Coming! Don't need to yell!' I yelled back downstairs. She could've just knocked and told me that dinner was ready like a normal person. Being a dysfunctional family is just exhausting sometimes. I thumped my way down the stairs to let Mum know I was ready for round two.

Mum looked at me judgingly like she always does – she likes to keep a cool exterior, but I know she's still seething on the inside. I shot her the same look right back. What can I say, I learnt from the best.

'I'm sorry for yelling . . . my darlings,' Mum exhaled. 'Please come and eat your dinner.'

I gave Mum a final look of disapproval as I swiped a plate of food. It's hard to get excited about a slow cooker dinner for the third time within the past two weeks.

I could sense Mum about to explode from behind me. She always sharply inhales just before she blows her top, though this time, Dad came to save the day. I don't know how he puts up with it, but he always manages to talk her down. He's good like that.

I wasn't going to stick around to find out if this was the time it failed. (I'd rather be on the comfy couch if Mum was going to rip my head off.)

The soap on the TV blared through the living room as I shovelled food into my mouth.

Nearly 6 pm. At least it's just about over, although James liked to watch his cartoons straight after. We all collectively groan when it starts, but at least it keeps James quiet for a bit.

James walked in front of the TV, sitting on the other side of the couch. He's learnt by now to stop invading my personal space – boy needs to shower more often. I looked up to see James staring at me while I ate my food.

'You made Mum cry,' James stated, staring daggers at me.

'You made Dad yell,' I replied sharply, shrugging my shoulders.

Nice try, buddy, we might be related but you'll never be quick enough to outwit me. You've still got a few years before you're too tall to talk down to, but for now, you're still gonna be the annoying little brother.

Eventually Mum and Dad joined us on the couch with their food, wearing obvious fake smiles to pretend like nothing was wrong. Dad sat between me and James. He reached over my lap to swipe the remote I had buried between my leg and the couch.

I scoffed as he flipped through the channels. He didn't even spare a thought that maybe I was watching something first. Not that there was anything good on anyway.

Buzz Buzz.

That was probably Zoe messaging me to find out whether I was able to smooth Mum over and go out tomorrow night. I pulled out my phone and started texting back.

hey girl, tomorrow is a bust. mum is on a rampage she could quite literally tear my head off –

'Mmm! So good, Mum!' James said suspiciously loudly.

Mum followed with an obvious fake cough. They were both trying to get my attention, I realised.

Mum looked pissed. Her eyebrows were saying more than enough to know that if I picked up that phone again, she would surgically insert it inside of me.

'Coming up next,' the woman on the TV reported, 'a new development in a string of mysterious deaths as another young victim has been found. More details after the br–'

The TV suddenly switched off. Dad still had the remote.

'So . . . how was school?' Dad asked.

'I was watching that,' James replied.

'Not anymore you're not. You don't need to hear about that,' Dad insisted.

'Why not, it's public television,' I cut in. I was in an argumentative mood since Dad had already turned off my show to begin with.

'Yeah, Dad, and I thought this was part of my screen time, you can't just turn –'

'Yes, I can!' Dad cut James off mid-sentence, hiding the remote under his thigh. 'If I say you're not watching it, then you're not watching!'

Dad was a shining example of 'Do as I say, not as I do'. He was never good at following rules, or his own for that matter. *Y'know what, I'm gonna tell him that.*

'Wow, Dad, how do you expect him to follow the rules when you can't,' I stated.

Mum gasped in shock.

Uh-oh. Here it comes.

'You do *not* talk to your father like that! Go to your room!' Mum bellowed.

'I –'

'No talking. Bedroom. Now.'

Fine. I didn't want to eat anyway, and I would've been more than happy to stay in my room in the first place. Mum was practically doing me a favour. I picked up my half-eaten plate and stormed into the kitchen, being as dramatic as I could so they wouldn't bother me again for the rest of the night. This family can only be taken in small doses, and I had reached my limit for the day.

I stomped back upstairs and slammed my door. Ahh, finally. Peace and quiet.

I went back to texting Zoe. I thought about sending her the message still half-typed on my keyboard, but I had a better idea.

y'know what, it's the craziest thing. Mum said yes! Will totally be there tomorrow. 100% wouldn't miss it for the world <3

A smirk crept across my face. What's the worst she could do, ground me? I bought this phone with my own allowance, so she'll have to pry it from my cold, dead, manicured nails.

If I get to go to this party, I'll gladly accept any punishment coming my way.

I settled back into my pillow and threw my headphones back on, scheduling everything I wanted to do tomorrow night with Zoe. It was gonna be the best night of our lives.

My alarm clock ticked over; 6:30 pm. Thirty minutes had passed in the blink of an eye. Zoe had gone to finish up her homework while I vacantly stared at the ceiling, listening to the playlist we had made together. *Let's Run Away* was a good title, she had picked it out. She's always been good at finding the perfect words to describe any scenario. It makes it easy to create memories with her. Meaningful ones.

As I silently mimed the lyrics to the music, a sharp crackle filled my left ear. I jerked my head to the side.

A sudden sting rang through my ear – guess that's what I get for having my music up so loud.

I lowered the volume. Strangely, the low music gave way to a buzzing sound. It was hard to tell whether it was the blood rushing through my throbbing ear or if there was something wrong with my headphones, but it was definitely there.

I slowly turned the volume back up, one pip at a time, straining my ears to hear the buzzing. It grew louder and louder, drowning out the song.

JAMES

Huh? I could faintly hear a voice speaking within the buzzing.

JAMES

James? Did I hear that right? Was that booger using a walkie-talkie with one of his friends or something? The volume reached its max capacity. Static filled my ears as I closed my eyes and searched for the voice.

JAMES

The voice boomed through the headphones. I ripped them off in fear. The ringing in my ears drowned out the sound as I rubbed my head, hoping the pain would go away. I was gonna teach that kid a lesson for messing with my stuff. He nearly burst my eardrums. I threw open my bedroom door.

'James! What the hell?' I yelled downstairs. I could hear the TV blaring cartoons. Why did he have the TV on so loud? It was much louder than any normal person could possibly need.

'James! James!' I shouted, stomping down the stairs. He probably couldn't hear me over the television; I could barely hear my own voice. The house was dark except for the hallway and the living room, where bright fluorescent lights bounced around the walls. As I got closer, I could hear James's voice. He was yelling.

. . . Something wasn't right.

I turned the corner and peeked my head inside the living room.

'Oh god, James! No!'

All the petty thoughts and feelings I had towards James, all the silly arguments and squabbles we had as siblings melted away as I stared in disbelief at the sight in front of me.

I ran over to James, who was twitching and convulsing on the floor.

'James!' I called out through tears, but I wasn't getting through to him. He couldn't hear me. I couldn't remember James ever having fits before. This was something new. I didn't know what to do. Reaching for the remote on the coffee table, I muted the television and threw it aside. I returned to James's side and desperately tried to shake him out of his episode.

'Mum! Dad! Where are you?!' James yelled.

Was it normal for people to speak during a seizure?

'Hello? Why are you all ignoring me?!' James continued, his voice cracking. Whatever he was going through and wherever he was right now, he sounded scared.

Panic crept in, and I felt useless. I needed help. I screamed with my entire being, as loudly as I could.

'M-Mum! Dad! Please, I need help!' My emotions began to overwhelm me. I wish I'd paid more attention during first-aid class. I heard the pitter-patter of Mum and Dad's feet come rushing down the stairs. They barged into the living room.

'Oh my god, James!'

'James, mate, what's wrong?!'

I could tell that they were starting to panic. We all gathered around James and tried our best to comfort him as he continued to writhe around.

'I came downstairs and found him like this. He's been calling out for you, but I don't think he can hear us,' I sniffled.

'Honey, call an ambulance!' Dad ordered Mum. She shuffled away into the kitchen, crying into the arm of her bathroom robe.

Dad swatted James's face hoping to knock him out of whatever was going on, but it was no use. James was buried deep inside whatever he was experiencing.

'Dad! Dad, thank god you're here,' James said.

I looked at Dad. That sentence alone was enough to break down his tough-dad exterior. Tears were rolling down his cheeks.

The dread and sheer helplessness inside me began to boil over as I watched Dad help James to no avail.

'What is happening? Please just look at me!' James screamed. The hurt in his voice sounded so real, like none of us could understand what he was experiencing.

This wasn't a seizure; this was something else.

Dad continued whispering into his ear, trying to help James get through his nightmare.

'Dad! Look at his eyes!' I yelled between trembles. James's eyes had rolled into the back of his head, leaving only white circles where his pupils used to be.

'Why are you doing this? I'm sorry. Please tell me you forgive me,' James continued. Nothing he was saying made any sense. It was separate from what was happening in the real world.

Dad continued crying and rambling, apologising over and over to James.

'It's all right, James, I forgive you. I forgive you. You've got nothing to worry about, Dad's not mad. Just please snap out of it.'

Mum came back into the room, the phone glued to her ear. She knelt next to Dad, stroking James's face.

'Please don't leave me,' James cried.

We all gathered around him, blubbering and crying as we tried our best to get through to James. Whatever we tried, nothing seemed to work. He couldn't see us, and he couldn't feel us comforting him.

I sat up and wiped my tears. James's face came into view and my worst fears came true.

'Dad! Look!' I yelled, pointing at James's face.

A stream of blood was running from James's nose down his cheek. This wasn't good.

I thought he was dying.

Dad fiercely shook James as Mum desperately wailed.

James's voice croaked as sounds and broken words escaped his mouth. None of it made any sense. Less than an hour ago, we were all sitting together eating dinner.

How did we get here?

I collapsed over James.

'I'm sorry. I'm sorry. I'm sorry. I'm sorry. I'm sorry. I'm sorry. I'm sorry. I'm sorry. I'm sorry,' I whispered over and over again.

A husky voice whispered into my ear. It was James. 'I don't know if you can hear me in there, Amy.'

My eyes lit up. He was talking to me. I couldn't tell if he could hear me or not, but James acknowledging my presence was enough to reduce me to a puddle of tears.

He gasped as he said his final words.

'. . . It's just you and me now.'

And then he stopped moving.

His words didn't make any sense. I never got any answers.

An ambulance came and took him away, but I don't think they were really paramedics.

They didn't try to revive him and they kept us away from his body.

His coffin was closed.

I wish I'd known that this was the last time I'd ever see you.

EMAIL RECEIVED!

FROM: <CONTACT@██████.COM>

WE APPRECIATE YOU FORWARDING THE ARCHIVE DOCUMENTS.

WE DO NOT APPRECIATE YOUR SILENCE.

WE WILL CONTINUE WITH CORRESPONDENCE FOR THE SAKE OF THE MISSION.
HOWEVER, WE WILL NOT FORGET.

THE LOG IMPLIES THE VICTIMS OF ANOMALY-991 LIVED OUT THEIR DEMISE IN A REALITY SEPARATE FROM OUR OWN, UNAWARE THAT THEIR ORIGINAL BODY IS DECEASED.

YOU ARE NOT THE ORIGINAL JANE.
YOU DIED.

BUT YOU SOMEHOW RETURNED IN YOUR ALTERNATE BODY.

HOW WAS THIS POSSIBLE?
WHAT IS THE PURPOSE OF THE BLACK SQUARE?

THE EXISTENCE OF THE ARCHIVES CONFIRMS ONE THING.
WHAT THE VICTIMS/YOU EXPERIENCED WAS REAL.
THESE EVENTS HAPPENED, BUT NOT IN THIS REALITY.

OUR SPECULATION WAS CORRECT.
ANOMALY-991 POSSESSES THE ABILITY TO TRAVEL BETWEEN REALITIES.
AS WELL AS THE ABILITY TO PULL PEOPLE THROUGH.
MENTALLY, NOT PHYSICALLY.

THEIR CONSCIOUSNESS IS TRANSFERRED TO THEIR OTHER BODY IN ANOTHER REALITY.
I EXPECT YOU HAVE A LOT OF QUESTIONS. AS DO WE.

WE ARE NOT THE ONLY ENTITIES SEEKING ANOMALY-991.

THE ANOMALY RESTRICTION COMMITTEE ARE ALSO SEARCHING.

THE ANOMALY RESTRICTION COMMITTEE HAVE A VERY FAR REACH.
FAR, FAR BEYOND THIS REALITY.
THEY POSSESS TECHNOLOGY TO ALSO TRAVEL BETWEEN WORLDS.
THE ARC EXISTS ACROSS THEM ALL.

THEY OBSERVE THE DOORS BETWEEN WORLDS.
THE HOLE IN THE WALL. THE REFLECTION IN THE MIRROR.
ALL POTENTIAL DOORS TO OTHER REALITIES.

THAT IS WHERE THE ANOMALIES ENTER.
THE ARC CONTAINS ANYONE AND ANYTHING THAT COMES THROUGH.
ANYTHING THAT DOESN'T BELONG IN THIS WORLD.

THIS IS THE REASON ANOMALY-991 WAS CONTAINED INSIDE THE ARC.

THERE IS ONLY ONE LOG LEFT.

IT MUST HAVE THE ANSWERS.

FIND THEM.

THE ARC LIVES,
FREEMAN.

THE EXTRA

ACT 1

This is the one, it has to be.

I look at the clock. The seconds tick by as if years are passing with each stroke.

I've sat in this room a thousand times memorising the pattern down to a science.

In exactly four seconds, the receptionist will sneeze, grab a tissue and head back to her desk.

. . .

'Achoo!'

Right on schedule.

Next, *he* is going to walk through that door with his cocky attitude and slicked-back hair. Except today, I have a feeling he isn't going to be feeling so hot.

I keep my smile concealed and patiently wait for the door to open.

Three . . . two . . . one.

The door swung open and a sweaty man hobbled through, desperately trying to catch his breath. The man's hair was unkempt, his crooked tie buried underneath an overcoat that had obviously never been touched by a lint roller. How . . . *imperfect.*

My buried smile cracked open as I watched the man carry himself over to the receptionist (who looked visibly repulsed by his appearance).

'Mr Harrington? You're late for your audition.'

The man wiped the beads of sweat from his forehead onto his sleeve, damaging the Italian cashmere with his putrid body fluids. *What a waste.*

'Hey, darlin'. Just do me a favour and let the boss know I'm here. He won't mind.'

The man followed his insipid attempt at charming the receptionist with a finger gun and a wink, both failing to impress.

'I'm sorry, Mr Harrington. You obviously look unwell, and we have to follow our safety procedures. I'm going to have to ask you to leave. I'll reschedule you for a later time,' the receptionist replied.

The man's smile dropped as his useless endeavours fell flat.

It's so easy. So predictable. Everything is going to plan.

How nonsensical I had been rehearsing my performance countless times, blind to the obvious truth that the reason I had failed time after time wasn't because of *me*, but because of him. It became easy enough to solve that problem.

Eliminate the competition.

Mr Harrington was a very predictable man.

He ate the same breakfast, showered at the same time, watched the same things.

I only had to rehearse three times before I knew what made this man tick.

Then all it took was a courtesy breakfast provided by yours truly, complete with a complimentary infectious disease.

A man with that much arrogance and ego would never say no to a free meal.

The air in the waiting room became static as the telephone rang out.

It's showtime.

'Mr Wake, the director is ready for you. Please head through the door and down the hallway,' the receptionist called.

I'd come to learn her name was Tiffany, but of course, I couldn't let her know I knew that.

I had rehearsed this moment countless times and had learnt a lot about her.

Mid-thirties, lives with her high school sweetheart, failed theatre school twice and took the closest opportunity she could to stay in her fantasy world, hoping one day, the director might happen to stumble across her mediocre talent. *Such a pity.*

I returned a polite nod and headed through the door. I knew this corridor and everyone in it well, and soon enough, I'd be face-to-face with the director. And this time, I was going to succeed.

No more rehearsals.

The dark space at the end of the hallway opened to the familiar theatre stage.

The director sat with his clipboard in the second row. I knew from rehearsing he was quietly doodling a picture of the man who'd performed before me, upset with his insultingly bad acting.

My shoes echoed against the stage floor as I walked over to my mark. I greeted the director with a subtle tip of my hat.

The director raised the clipboard to his face. 'Nicholas Wake, auditioning for the role of Audrey's neighbour, also known as Bowler Hat Man, for season five of *Lovely Day*. Whenever you're ready.'

Any normal actor would've been rattled with nerves auditioning in front of a renowned director, but I had re-lived this moment an infinite number of times, each with an infinite number of possible outcomes. By now, I felt more like the character than I did myself.

My mannerisms had become his, his words were my own.

I was going to get the part, whether they knew it or not.

With a tip of my hat, I began my performance.

I flicked the lights on in my apartment, illuminating the living room with a bleak hue. It had been a few hours since the audition. From doing many rehearsals, I knew I wouldn't hear back until tomorrow at the earliest.

Though who knows, this time could be different.

I pulled off my rain-soaked clothes, staring at myself in the reflection.

I have done it; I've found the right world.

It was too soon to celebrate, but I had a good feeling about this one.

Exhaustion claimed me as I collapsed onto the bed, thinking about the possibilities I perhaps didn't account for.

Could I have missed something?

Countless rehearsals had left a scar of anxiety etched into my mind. This wasn't the first time I had thought I'd found the one, only to wind up in yet another rehearsal.

Rehearsal. Rehearsal. Rehearsal.

The word had become so familiar to me that I'd forgotten for everyone else it had an entirely different, less complex meaning. It's always been a natural ability since I was a child.

Like everyone else has the ability to smell, touch, taste and feel, I have the ability to *rehearse*.

To go backwards, forwards and sideways.

In time. In space.

However I please.

The proscenium arch: the space between the stage and the real world. I could travel freely through it.

The earliest rehearsal I can recall was getting scolded by my mother for starting Christmas too early. I stayed up all night opening every present until the room was littered with brightly coloured paper.

It was the happiest moment I had felt in my young life.

Mother didn't agree.

She yelled and screamed that I had ruined Christmas. I didn't understand why she wasn't happy. The presents were for me.

I spent Christmas Day locked in my room with nothing. No toys to play with, no television to watch. Just me and my thoughts.

I thought a lot that day, about what I could have done differently. I remember closing my eyes and thinking about an alternate outcome. If I stayed in my room that night and waited until my mother was awake.

I could see it so clearly in my head. The longer I thought about that other reality, the clearer it became in my mind. The blurriness faded and the noise of that world became vivid.

I opened my eyes, *and there it was.*

The world in my head suddenly lay before me.

I was back in my bedroom, underneath the warm, layered blankets while everyone slept.

I tiptoed to the living room to find the presents back under the tree, still wrapped as if they had never been touched.

I had been given a second chance. A do-over. As if the world before were simply . . . *a rehearsal.*

The ability became stronger as I got older.

I could travel to and from realities as I pleased, yet one peculiarity I had come to notice was that I existed across all of them as a singular entity.

The world would not allow for there to be two of me in the one reality.

I vividly remember reliving an old childhood memory once I had reached adulthood.

Memories are a fickle thing. You can never quite remember exactly how it happened, and your mind tends to fill in the blanks.

The world of my memory was similar, yet different. It was as if I had incorrectly remembered details from that moment, yet somewhere in space and time, this version of my memory existed as its own world, just as real as the one I had lived.

Even more perplexing, I didn't relive the memory again through the eyes of a child, but instead as a bystander in my adult body.

In a blip, the younger version of myself had disappeared from existence.

I had overwritten his presence simply by being in this world.

I witnessed the horror in my parents' eyes as their little boy was erased in front of them.

I couldn't simply explain that I was their child from the future, nor could I explain why I was in their house, and so I travelled back to my own world, uneasy with the chaos I had created.

An innocent mistake that would become my first casualty. The first of many other versions of me that had been erased.

I remember telling Mother about rehearsals. She didn't understand, how could she?

I thought the best way to explain it was to show her, to take her with me to another world. One where Father was alive again, one where they hadn't met yet. She wanted to fall in love all over again. That's what she truly wanted.

It made me happy to see her happy. It had been years since she had seen him.

I visited Father frequently whenever I pleased, knowing that doing so would erase that version of me from his world, leaving great pain whenever I left.

In every world, he always ended up dying. Sometimes the same way, and other times, differently. The universe always caught up eventually.

I wish he didn't check his watch so often and simply enjoyed the world around him.

It was easier to rationalise the pain he felt knowing he wouldn't feel it for too long.

Constants and variables. Some things are fated to happen.

Though I couldn't help but be a little selfish.

There was an infinite amount of him, there was only one of me. One *real* me.

Mother wanted to stay in that world forever, even if it meant that I never existed.

I didn't blame her; I know I wasn't easy. She was happy, and that was enough.

I couldn't say the same for my mother back in our original world.

I returned and found her on the floor with blood pouring from her nose.

It seemed that she couldn't travel the same way I could. I had pulled her mind with me, leaving her body to rot back in her original world.

She muttered incoherent sentences as she writhed on the floor, but she sounded happy.

Then she was dead.

She was where she belonged, and I was to return to a world with no parents.

Call it homesick, call it an unspoken connection, but I wanted to stay in a world where I existed. I didn't want to be an anomaly living outside my own existence. And so, I stayed.

No parents, no guidance. I was free to wander through realities, building whatever path I wanted.

But no matter how much freedom I had gained, I had lost a family. I was alone.

The anguish forced my eyes back open. It was still dark in my apartment, and an hour had passed as I had swum around lost in my memories.

There wasn't much else to do; I had done everything I could.

This is the one, it has to be.

Tick . . . Tick . . . Tick . . . Tick.

I sat at the end of the bed with my feet perfectly aligned as seconds turned into hours. There wasn't anything to do besides wait for a phone call.

There was no reason to shower and prepare for the day, yet I did it anyway.

The rehearsals all led to this day that I had lived a hundred times, yet I had a feeling it would be different this time. Something deep in my core told me.

Ring . . . Ring . . .

I let it ring out a few times to not seem overly eager.

'Hello.'

'Oh, hello, sir, this is Tiffany from Lovely Studios. I'm just calling to congratulate you. You've got the part.'

'That is . . . wonderful news,' I replied.

'We've got you down as a recurring character for season five and casting really came down to the wire, so shooting will start in two weeks. Please don't be late.'

'See you then.'

Click.

The weeks following the phone call became a blur as I became my character.

I had been replaced with the happy-go-lucky, kind neighbour who lived a homely life with his wife and two children.

His life was a stark contrast from my own, but something about that life resonated with me.

He lived in a world where nothing went wrong. There was no need for rehearsals or do-overs because nothing bad ever happened.

No fathers destined to die. No rotting mothers.

It was going to be me and my two children, and I would protect and teach them.

I would greet the neighbours and invite Audrey over for dinner.

I'll have the family I always wanted. That will be my story.

ACT 2

The cab ride to the studio was accompanied by a static quality to the air. I ran through every possibility in my head, pondering how many rehearsals lay ahead.

I wasn't going to risk any chances of failure, though I would have to use it sparingly.

My body continues to naturally age throughout each rehearsal, and I suppose it would look quite strange if I had aged ten years in the span of a few months.

The cab came to a stop outside the studio's entrance.

I stepped out and couldn't help but stare at the building in front of me.

The web of possibilities and outcomes overlapped in my mind, sending visions of other worlds flashing across my eyes. It was something that rarely happened, but I certainly remember the feeling.

The feeling of a divergence: an important event that creates a fork in the road of life. A single moment can drastically alter the course of life, and this moment was fast approaching.

A shrill woman suddenly burst through the studio doors.

'You're late! We've been looking for you!' the woman scowled.

'We've been trying to call you! I *sincerely* hope you received our message,' she continued.

A foreign twang of anxiety danced along my spine.

I'd switched my phone off for the past few days. I wasn't expecting a change of plans and distractions were a hindrance to my focus. Though whatever they needed to tell me, it felt important.

I couldn't allow this kind of first impression before I had even begun. I needed to change it.

I closed my eyes and visualised my apartment. Exactly as it was.

I opened my eyes and found myself in the living room, staring at myself in the mirror.

This moment was familiar – it was two days before I left for the studio. I hoped that this was early enough to answer the call.

Ring . . . Ring . . .

I wasn't going to hesitate to answer this time.

It was the receptionist. What was so important that she would be calling me so soon?

'Oh, hello. This is Tiffany from Lovely Studios.'

I impatiently waited for the receptionist to get to the point of the call.

'Mr Wake, I'm afraid I have some unfortunate news.'

. . .

. . .

. . .

. . .

Click.

How *dare* they.

How could they do this to *me*? Reducing me to an extra.

They cut me out of the story, *my story*.

That's why I had been late, the call-time for extras was earlier than the rest.

They can't do this to me.

They can't take my family away from me, after everything that I've done.

I closed my eyes and tried to find it. The world where this never happens.

But all I could see was black. Never-ending darkness inside my eyelids.

I can't change this. I can't rehearse this.

This is how it was meant to be.

The cab ride felt different the second time around. The air no longer had a vibrance to it, instead an inescapable staleness wafted around me. The cab pulled up and I stepped outside, looking up at the studio.

It was the same, but different. Or rather, it was me that had changed.

'Hello, Mr Wake. Right on schedule.'

The same shrill woman greeted me at the studio door, although with a different tone. There was no reason for her to rush me since I wasn't late. I had shown up to their miserable call for the extras right on time.

I could feel my mask starting to slip as I followed the woman through the studio, my true feelings of disgust and hatred peeking through my neutral exterior.

They took what was mine and I would neither forgive nor forget.

If only they knew what I was capable of.

How much sorrow and pain I could inflict on every single person in this building without breaking a sweat. But for now, I knew I must behave. The divergence was fast approaching, and who knows what it had in store for me.

The woman sat me down in a chair in a busy room as people danced around applying make-up and fitting me with the clothes I had come to love. A slim, tan-checkered suit with a bowler hat.

It was perfect.

Slipping into the suit only magnified the callous emotions that were boiling inside me.

The Bowler Hat Man had had a perfect family and lived in a perfect town.

But now he was just the man at the bus stop.

He deserved better than that. I deserved more.

A man with an abrasive air about him stormed into the room, barking orders at everyone before snapping his fingers at me to follow him.

'You've got one line, here's the script. Don't stuff it up, we all want to go home.'

I flipped through the pages to find my one pathetic line highlighted in yellow.

'The world's your oyster, little lady.'

How miserable.

The man walked ahead and pushed open the double doors, revealing an expansive, vibrant and colourful world of plastic grass and painted skies. It perfectly captured the feeling of stepping into an entirely different world – a doorway to the world I longed to live in.

The leading lady caught my eye from behind the crossing of people shuffling by. I had seen her on television, but the images that she conjured in my mind seemed to come from somewhere else.

It was a peripheral memory, though I had no recollection of meeting her before.

'Where's the extra?! Find him and get him on set!' the director barked into his megaphone.

A sea of eyes looked in my direction as I walked closer. They were waiting for me, staring daggers as I walked down the street and sat on the bench with the young woman sitting on the far end. She seemed more uncaring than on television.

It was her.

Audrey.

Watching her from across the bench, I felt a sharp sadness as I mourned a relationship that would never be. My longing to play the part of a doting father in a happy family was minimised to one conversation with this girl.

I gave a subtle wave to try to catch her attention, but her downturned eyes suggested she wasn't interested in talking. I leant a little closer while the director was busy speaking to his assistants.

'Audrey . . . you're a very lucky girl to be here,' I said, trying to stay calm, while my emotions inside me rampaged. I couldn't quite tell if what I was feeling was sadness, jealousy or hatred.

I waited . . . and waited for Audrey's answer as I spoke, but she never responded.

Audrey continued staring down at her feet, uninterested in what I had to say.

She didn't move an inch to even acknowledge my presence, instead choosing to face the other way. There was little possibility that she didn't hear me speak.

. . .

. . .

. . .

What a rude girl.

'Quiet on set!' the director barked again. I quietly leant back in my seat, unimpressed by her ignorance.

Rudeness isn't a quality that belongs in this world.

The feelings of affection quickly dissipated, leaving me hollow.

The entire street went quiet as the director raised his megaphone.

'And . . . action!'

The girl I remembered from television popped into existence and sat up straight, bright and cheery without a care in the world.

And then she began to speak.

'I wonder where life –'

Then she suddenly stopped, startled by something. She looked almost horrified.

Audrey seemed catatonic, as if stuck somewhere deep within her own mind. She began to shake uncontrollably.

I cracked a wide smile at Audrey, hiding the malice I truly felt, to ease her discomfort. The last thing I wanted was her to make a scene.

I reached out and placed my hand on her shoulder, and Audrey began to scream an ear-piercing screech that ruptured out of her like a lightning bolt.

Panic set in as the cast and crew all gawked at the scene.

Without a moment of hesitation Audrey leapt from her seat towards me, screaming as she raised her pointed nails.

Audrey threw her entire weight onto me, bowling me over onto the concrete pavement. I felt her nails dig into my face. She began clawing like a ferocious animal fighting for her life.

My own cries became mixed with hers as I shielded my face. I desperately tried to open my eyes in between her swipes, only to see a red cloud blurring my vision.

She was drawing blood with each blow, the colour of her nails a thick layer of red.

I tried to push her off, but her instinctual strength and speed was overpowering.

I had to get out of here. It didn't matter how.

Amid the chaos, I closed my eyes and pictured my apartment. Blood began to pool in my eye sockets.

I focused on the apartment as it became clearer and the screaming started to dim.

I opened my eyes, and I was back.

My face felt hot as I touched my cheeks, and I noticed a flow of blood running down my fingers. I looked into the mirror behind me.

My face. *What has she done to my face?*

It was ruined.

Long red cuts streamed across ear to ear. They were deep and stung.

I couldn't stand to look at myself. My hand, balled into a fist, lurched out of its own will and collided with the mirror, splintering the hideous reflection staring back at me.

That girl.

I had done nothing to provoke her, yet she tried to end my life.

In a way, she had.

I couldn't undo this. I couldn't rehearse this.

All that was left was to look at the monster staring back at me.

I stared and stared as the features of my face started to fade.

I could feel the hatred of every one of me all at once. Their malice became my will.

Past, present and future attempts at happiness, all for nothing. Erased forever.

It became impossible to distinguish where my mouth was, where my eyes sat. They bled into one another until all that was left was a blurry memory of what I once looked like.

I just wanted my moment of happiness.

I just wanted a family again.

Gone.

I needed to know why.

I opened my eyes and was outside Audrey's window.

She sat in front of the mirror, completely still. Her face in the reflection looked upset. I watched from outside as she raised an arm into the air, bringing it down against her other arm, over and over.

An older woman burst through the door and tried to stop her, crying hysterically as Audrey fought back and pushed her out of the room, locking it.

I didn't quite understand what I was seeing, nor did I really care.

For a moment, Audrey noticed me standing outside. I thought little of the possibility that she could see me against the darkness, but those wide blue eyes said otherwise.

It didn't matter, I would be gone before she had time to comprehend what she had seen.

There was no reason for me to be here any longer. There were no answers here.

I pictured a different moment in time and blinked over and over as if switching channels on the television. Brief moments of Audrey's life flashed by.

Countless days, backwards and forwards through time waiting and watching, looking for an answer to no avail.

Audrey noticed my presence in some, and in others I was just an observer, futilely looking for a moment that seemed to have never occurred. Nothing stood out as the reason for Audrey's raw hatred for me. I considered the endeavour a lost cause until I stumbled across a curious moment.

The curtains were drawn. I couldn't see what was happening inside, but I could still hear Audrey's voice.

'The story is about me. I don't want more people!' she barked.

She was on the phone to somebody, sounding agitated.

'I want you to cut them: the neighbours. Cut the whole storyline.'

. . .

'This is my story! My home! Don't take this away from me.'

. . .

'Don't call me Jane! You know I hate that! Just do it!'

Beep

. . .

It was you. You took it from me.

All because of your own selfishness.

All because of *you*.

There was nothing. No answer. No reason. You destroyed me, for nothing.

Children.

Selfish, monstrous children.

All I wanted was to be happy.

All I wanted was a family.

After everything, I feel I deserved that.

After watching Father die over and over.

After watching Mother writhe on the floor, knowing she was happier elsewhere without my existence.

After a lifetime of despair, feeling out of place in this world, I feel I deserved that.

If that world must remain out of reach, *it felt only reasonable to return the favour.*

Children. Parents. Grandparents. Families.

All of them selfishly taking for granted what it means to be cherished by others.

But they'll soon know.

They'll know my pain.

They'll know what it's like to live in despair.

They'll know what a real living nightmare feels like.

I could've erased Audrey right where she stood, but I had a more appropriate idea.

Audrey wasn't going to die alone in her bedroom, no.

She was going to die in front of the people she called family, all the while wandering through her own personal hell.

That's what she deserved.

I closed my eyes and pictured the studio. The place where it happened. The world around me became loud as the burning sensation returned to my face, and the healed scars reopened. People gathered around Audrey, pinning her to the ground as she thrashed about.

This was my opportunity. I was going to take her somewhere faraway.

'It's him! It's him!' Audrey cried as her struggles to break free became useless.

I closed my eyes and focused on Audrey.

Infinite worlds flicked across my eyes, and I saw every possibility for every life she could live. I could hear her voice inside my head, as if I were narrating her life.

A vision of the world began to form, a familiar yet dreamlike reality of the place she called home.

Only, this world was not meant to protect Audrey.

It was going to torture her, where she would become a prisoner of her own memories.

The air began to change and the chaos dissipated, leaving me and Audrey alone in the medical bay. I fell back as my body – still reeling from the attack moments ago – struggled to compose itself. I had done it.

In a few moments, Audrey was going to awaken in a world that she had brought upon herself. A familiar world that would ultimately cause her to spiral into despair.

Satisfaction swelled within me. I was content with my revenge.

It felt right. I had done the right thing.

Audrey lay unconscious on the bed, completely oblivious that her original body had already started to decompose. I debated observing Audrey as she began losing her mind, but I had plenty of time for that. I was more curious about what lay ahead for her. This world meant much more to me than it ever would to her.

Don't have too much fun without me.

The astroturf crunched against my shoes as I strolled through the road admiring the picturesque houses.

Every house was furnished as a home yet was void of inhabitants. A blank slate for me to create my own world.

It was perfect. *A world where nothing bad ever happens.*

I kept walking until eventually there was nothing besides grass and sky as far as the eye could see.

It was beautiful. This was my reward.

For every little piece of my pain I shared with others, the world felt a little brighter.

I felt understood.

I didn't know how long I was going to walk; maybe forever, or perhaps when I found a reason to stop. Eventually, I found one.

A crossroads forked through the road stretching out in different directions, accompanied by a small house nestled in the corner. I knocked on the door, curious by its existence in the middle of nothing. Nobody answered.

Welcome Home sprawled across the doormat. I took the house up on its invitation and let myself inside. The interior was peculiar yet familiar, contrasting with the innards of the houses back in the neighbourhood.

The living room was absent of any furniture besides a single armchair facing a small television. The screen flickered with monochrome static that quietly wafted through the room.

I turned the doorknob to a small room squashed with furniture. An awkwardly large bed filled the space, leaving a small walkway to a desk tucked away next to a bookshelf.

A small diary caught my attention. It looked weathered and used. A title was penned on a piece of tape:

Archives of Despair.

I sat down and flicked through the pages.

Flat . . . Grandma? . . .

Pretend People? . . .

. . . How peculiar.

The diary was filled from end-to-end with stories detailing numerous victims' accounts. All of them shared something in common. A sighting of someone referred to as *The Bowler Hat Man.*

Were these stories . . . about me?

I had no memory of these events ever occurring, yet they seemed to be written in such complex detail that it didn't seem right to dismiss them as fiction.

I couldn't quite decide until I noticed a distinctive detail that would prove beyond doubt that these stories were indeed real.

My handwriting.

Somehow, I had written these stories . . .

I felt a sharp sensation in my temple as I desperately tried to wrap my head around what I was looking at. These diary entries were without a doubt written by my own hand, but I couldn't recall writing them. There was only one explanation that made everything make sense.

I had been here before sometime in the future and called this place home.

These accounts were about me in a distant future where that feeling of revenge, despair and of needing others to feel my pain had never subsided. I'd continued the pattern to satiate my appetite.

Today was the first time I had felt it. That momentary rush of sweet bliss as I pulled Audrey into her own personal nightmare.

The rush of endorphins releasing knowing that somebody, *somebody* had experienced the otherworldly torment I had endured.

But it certainly wouldn't be the last.

Certainly not now since I had been kind enough to turn my victims into stories. Stories that already had an ending of despair. All I had to do was read along.

The connection I felt with Audrey as I pulled her though and heard her voice inside my head as if she were narrating her own life.

It all made sense.

I had written all those thoughts down here, in the *Archives of Despair.*

I always did have a knack for the theatrics.

I smiled as I grabbed another diary off the shelf and violently flipped through the pages.

Smile Street . . .

The Neighbours' Cat . . .

New Shoes . . .

Hundreds of diaries with countless entries all detailing the various ways I had pulled children from their reality and placed them in their own exclusive purgatory.

Who would've known the anger and jealousy I had directed towards Audrey was only the tip of the iceberg. She had opened the floodgates and introduced me to a world that wasn't so bad.

A world that got a little brighter each time I shared a part of myself.

I had acquired all the knowledge I needed to feed my appetite and continue the cycle.

I suppose I should thank you, Audrey.

For helping me find my purpose.

For pushing the divergence in the right direction.

For helping me discover my true identity.

I leave you this reality as a thank you for all the ache and misery you gave me.

Without you, none of this would've been possible.

I truly hope this world breaks your spirit, just as you did mine.

See you 'round, neighbour.

ANOMALY RESTRICTION COMMITTEE - EMPLOYEE RECORD #475

TITLE: DR

FULL NAME: WAKE, ROBERT

AGE: 41 (UPDATE: DECEASED)

CHILDREN: WAKE, NICHOLAS

ADDRESS: [redacted]

PASSPORT NO: [redacted]

EMPLOYEE NO: #[redacted]

DEPARTMENT: LEVEL 5 RESEARCH AND DEVELOPMENT

ROLE: CHIEF RESEARCH OFFICER

YEARS ACTIVE: 1993-2011

REPORTING SUPERIOR: DR [redacted]

NOTABLE PROJECTS:

(1994-1997)

Extended research and development as Junior Scientist on **OPERATION WORMHOLE**. Studied and reported the various effects of cross-world travel on the human body. Schematics for VERSION 0.81 of world travel hardware provided by Dr Wake and used as a blueprint for VERSION 1.0.

(2003-2005)

Development of communication technology originally harvested from WORLD-082. Technology found in its infancy and used as a blueprint to create a private projection that only the intended individual can observe.

ADDITIONAL NOTES:
Following Dr Wake's contribution to **OPERATION WORMHOLE**, Dr Wake has been chosen as Prime Candidate for the role of CHIEF RESEARCH OFFICER due to outstanding commitment to cross-world travel research by providing his child as a live human subject for research and testing purposes.

To show appreciation for Dr Wake's generous contribution to the Research and Development Department of the Anomaly Restriction Committee, a complimentary fruit basket has been sent to his wife.

2011 UPDATE: Following the catastrophic failure of several unlicensed experiments undertaken by Dr Robert Wake, funding has been permanently revoked for all future endeavours and Dr Wake is hereby stripped of his title at ARC. Upon termination, Dr Wake was equipped with a Death Day Watch that will remain on his person until the clock expires, resulting in his death across every timeline.

THIS INFORMATION IS CLASSIFIED AND MUST NOT BE REPRODUCED.

INTERNAL VOICE CALL RECORD

DATE RECORDED: ██/██/████ 7.42 PM
CALL LENGTH: 0m 55s
TRANSMITTING NO:████████
RECEIVING NO:████████

DIAL TONE

'This is outside business hours, so it better be important.'

'Sir, this is Dr ██████, we've just had an urgent report come through from the Security Department.'

'Okay, son. What is it? My dinner is getting cold.'

'Sir, the recon team leading the observation of Anomaly-991's base of operations on WORLD-1492 have discovered several documents detailing victims of illegal world travel.'

'Son, this isn't urgent news.'

'There's more, sir. The recon team left their point of world entry open since Anomaly-991 was not present and no threats were detected.'

'That's against protocol, you need to report this immediately to the superior overlooking the –'

'Sir! Two signatures have been recorded entering the doorway.'

'I'm sorry, did you say *two* individuals? They're inside the ARC?'

'Yes, sir, one has been accounted for: a young girl is currently in temporary holding. The other's location is unknown.'

'Son, listen very carefully. Wipe the girl's memory, she must not remember anything about the inside of this building. As for Anomaly-991, put the building on lockdown. This is a level five threat. Anomaly-991 is somewhere in the facility.'

'He's . . . he's here? Oh god. I- . . . I'll inform the chief of security.'

'Once he has been captured, release the girl.'

'Yes, sir.'

CALL ENDED

EMAIL RECEIVED!

FROM: <FREEMAN@████████.COM

OUR RECORDS SHOW ANOMALY-991 WAS CAPTURED FOLLOWING HIS ENTRY INTO THE ANOMALY RESTRICTION COMMITTEE.
HOWEVER, ANOMALY-991'S IMPRISONMENT WAS SHORT-LIVED HAVING ESCAPED SEVERAL DAYS LATER AND FREEING SEVERAL ANOMALIES IN THE PROCESS.
WE HOPE YOUR QUESTIONS HAVE SUFFICIENTLY BEEN ANSWERED.
UNFORTUNATELY, OURS HAVE NOT.

THIS ENDS OUR WORKING RELATIONSHIP, HOWEVER WE STILL REQUEST YOUR COOPERATION WITH FURTHER RESEARCH.
THE REVELATION THAT YOU HAVE VENTURED INSIDE THE ANOMALY RESTRICTION COMMITTEE IS MOST ENLIGHTENING TO OUR CAUSE.

THE INFORMATION DORMANT IN YOUR BRAIN IS TOO VALUABLE TO BE LEFT TO DECAY.
WE POSSESS SUFFICIENT TECHNOLOGY TO HARVEST THIS INFORMATION AND WOULD APPRECIATE YOUR ASSISTANCE.

THE CLEANER IS EN ROUTE TO YOUR POSITION.
DO NOT ATTEMPT TO RESIST.

ASSUME A LYING POSITION WITH YOUR HANDS AND FEET TOGETHER.

THE CLEANER WILL USE FORCE IF NECESSARY.

WE AT THE FREEDOM FOR ANOMALOUS BEINGS' ASSOCIATION LOOK FORWARD TO YOUR ARRIVAL.

FREEMAN

NOT SCARED ENOUGH?

THE NIGHTMARE CONTINUES IN CALEB FINN'S NEXT BOOK ...

NEED HELP?

If you're going through a tough situation that you don't feel comfortable talking about with your friends or family, you can find help elsewhere. Reach out to a counsellor on a free anonymous hotline or website.

AUSTRALIA

Kids Helpline: 1800 55 1800 / kidshelpline.com.au

Free, private and confidential 24-hour phone and online counselling service for young people aged 5 to 25. You can call any time, for any reason.

NEW ZEALAND

0800 What's Up: 0800 942 8787

Mon–Sun 11am–11pm / whatsup.co.nz

Free counselling helpline and webchat service for children and teenagers.

ACKNOWLEDGEMENTS

To my darling partner,
Thank you for your infinite patience.
You are my missing piece,
My other half,
My happy ending.

To my incredible fans,
It's been a long journey together.
From making spooky videos in my bedroom,
To publishing my own spooky book.
We finally made it.
Thank you.

And to everyone at Penguin Random House,
Thank you for seeing something in me.
For taking a shot on the weird kid.
Your guidance and knowledge were invaluable.

I love you all.

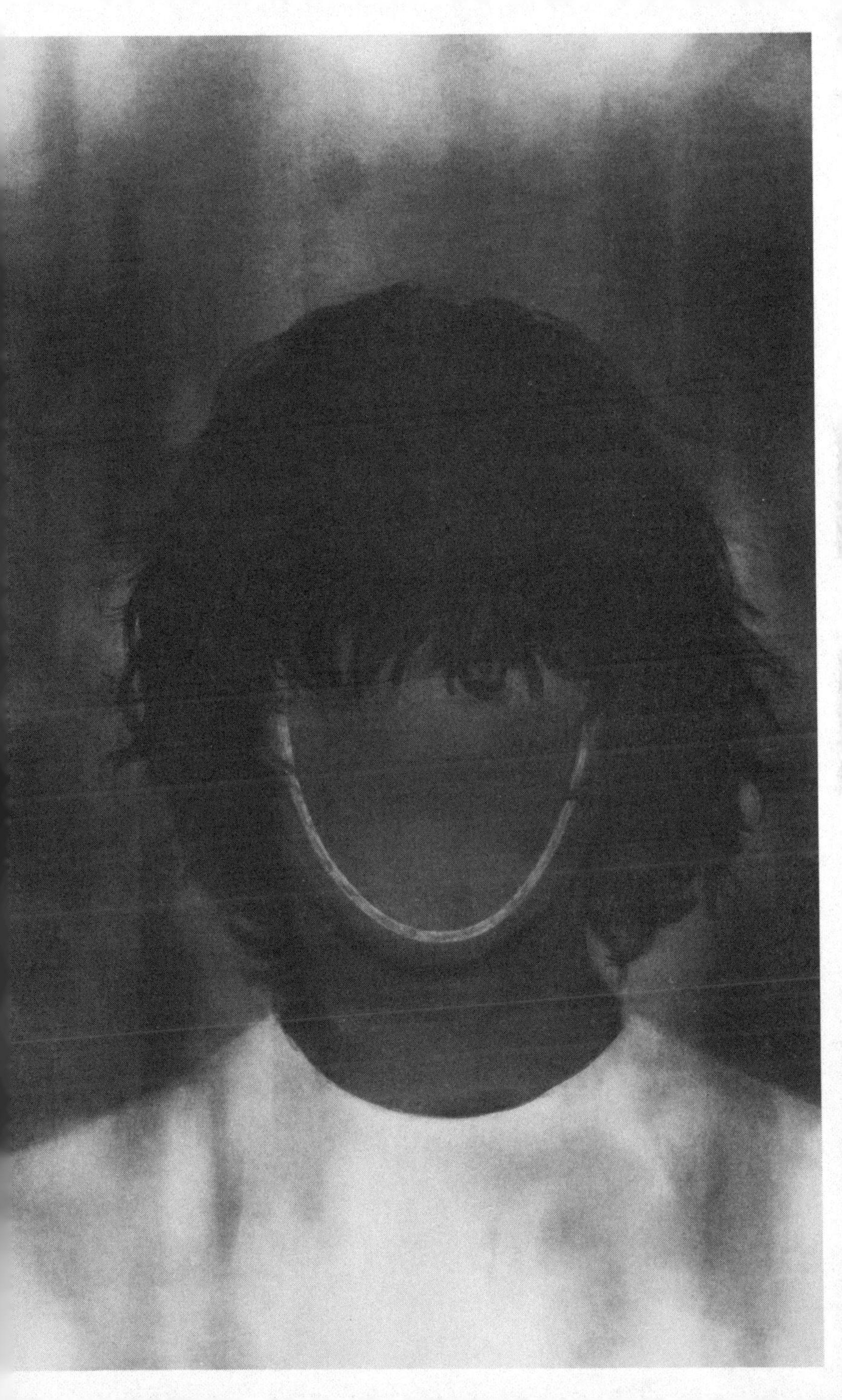

ABOUT THE AUTHOR

Caleb Finn is Australia's most-followed male content creator, with over 17 million fans worldwide. Known for his cinematic short horror films, Caleb is inspired by film, digital culture, body horror and liminal spaces. His fascination with *creepypastas*, urban legends found in the corners of the online world, motivated him to write his own collection of scary short stories. He documents his parenthood journey on his TikTok channel to millions of followers.

Caleb lives in Melbourne with his partner and young child. *Archives of Despair* is his debut novel.

ABOUT THE ILLUSTRATOR

New Zealand born, Melbourne based artist Adam Parata is known for his atmospheric and thought-provoking work. Drawing inspiration primarily from life and the complexity of the human experience, Adam's handling of visual storytelling can be described as a dance of both literal and abstract forms to communicate simple and complex messages. This sensitive approach to handling form, detail, light and texture is where the magic lives, and it's through these focused sensibilities that Adam is able to create drama, story and atmosphere in his masterful work.

Adam finds working with darker themes to be most thought-provoking, and what interests him the most about illustration is its ability to tell stories, share and communicate at scale.

For me, the work should ideally transcend itself and become a portal to a story, an experience, another world, another time.

This is the power of the arts; it's like magic.

Growing up studying the masters, watching films, playing sport, obsessing over video games and building huts in the countryside of New Zealand has no doubt informed Adam's work. But it's this merging of a curious country boy feeding on the offerings of a modern city that continues to grow the fruits of Adam's labour.

Q&A WITH CALEB FINN

Congratulations on writing your first novel. How did you first come up with the idea for *Archives of Despair*?

Thank you! It's been a lifelong dream of mine to write horror short stories.

Archives of Despair was first born from the idea of what *Scary Stories to Tell in the Dark* would look like in 2023. Kids are a lot harder to scare these days, and a lot has changed over the years since frightening scarecrows and witches in the woods were the pinnacle of terror.

The internet and its creepypastas and urban legends were a huge inspiration for me.

What was your writing process like for *Archives of Despair?* Did you have a writing routine, or any regular rituals?

It was a fantastic experience. Recalling all of my childhood fears and nightmares was thrilling as well as very confronting. I believe that true horror happens close to home, which is why most of the stories in *Archives of Despair* happen in very normal, everyday environments.

It was a little tricky to balance writing an entire book while caring for my one-year-old son and making daily content for the internet! Once I got into the groove, it became hard to stop. I loved every second of it.

I had a very strict ritual for the process. I listened to two very specific YouTube playlists every single time I sat down to write: *The Caretaker – Everywhere At The End of Time* and *Silent Chill* (a relaxing playlist from the soundtrack of *Silent Hill*). Definitely recommend listening while reading!

How long have you been working on it?

I think just about a year, if you include all the pre-planning as well as the countless rewrites and proofreads (haha).

Do you have a favourite book? Have you always been inspired by horror?

My favourite book would have to be *Uzumaki* by Junji Ito. He's an incredible horror manga artist. I would have to say *The Enigma of Amigara Fault* by the same author is my all-time favourite short story. Truly terrifying.

Horror has always been a huge inspiration for me since I was little. I was a spooky kid. Horror just has this mysterious and cosmic draw that pulls me in. I really do find comfort in the dark.

What inspired you to become a writer?

I've been making horror content in short video formats for six years; it's my bread and butter. Though I really wanted to challenge myself and bring my point of view into an entirely new space.

I had to completely rethink my entire approach since I couldn't visually scare the viewer anymore – I had to describe it. I'd have to say now I prefer the latter.

Do you think there is a place for comedy in horror writing? R.L. Stine once said, 'laughing and being scared, I think is the same visceral reaction.' Do you agree?

Absolutely. Horror takes form in all shapes and sizes. Being happy and terrified are on the opposite ends of the spectrum, and it takes a very skilled storyteller to make the two ends meet. Jordan Peele's films are a fantastic example of how to combine the two to tell incredible stories.

What surprised you most about the publishing process?

TIME. IT TAKES SO MUCH TIME. I really thought I could smash out a quick twenty pages a day. Oh, ho ho! How innocent I was.

What did you want to be when you grew up?

I wanted to be a video game tester (haha). I really thought it was just being paid to play games all the time. Instead, it's searching for bugs and glitches for eight hours a day and not actually playing.

I did end up becoming a preschool teacher for about six years. Kids are just endlessly fascinating to watch as they learn things and expand their understanding of the world.

Being a content creator and now a published author of children's horror books was definitely not on my bingo card, but I couldn't imagine my life any other way.

Do you have any tips for aspiring authors?

Any and every idea that floats through your head: WRITE. IT. DOWN.

Originally, I had about thirty stories planned out for *Archives of Despair* before I nailed it down to ten. I still have my notepad with the most ridiculous stories I made up from just observing our world and thinking how I could twist it into a nightmare. I remember I had a story about a kid who saw the neighbours' cat transform into an old man in a leotard! Pretty scary stuff.

What are you most afraid of?

Mannequins and aliens.